MISTS OF THE COUCHSACRAGE

Rescue From State Land

"A novel of the Adirondacks, possibly in the not too distant future."

By

Alden L. Dumas

ISBN: 1-4107-7967-X (e-book)
ISBN: 1-4107-7966-1 (Paperback)
ISBN: 1-4107-7965-3 (Dust Jacket)

Library of Congress Control Number: 2003095256

This book is printed on acid free paper.

Printed in the United States of America
Bloomington, IN

1stBooks - rev. 11/17/03

Dedication

"The Mists of the Couchsacrage" is dedicated to all early settlers of the Adirondacks, and any descendants who have lost their family's camps and land-use rights due to policies and practices beyond their control.

<u>Prologue</u>

Legends have it that "Couchsacrage" (Cooch-aw-crawge) is an Algonkian name; used when those of that noble tribe of Native Americans referred to much of what we now call the Adirondack State Park as a "dismal wilderness," or, in their language, "the couchsacrage."

The land was not productive enough to sustain human settlement for long. There was not enough edible plant life, nor an abundance of wild game to provide meat for long standing villages. The Native Americans usually just crossed through this place, if they entered it at all. Anyone trying to exist here for long would usually find himself to be desperate for food, and generally very miserable, if indeed he didn't die from insect bites, hunger, sickness, or hypothermia.

The Iroquois looked with great disfavor on one foolhardy enough to try and survive in the Couchsacrage. They derisively called such adventurers "rat-i-ron-taks," or "bark-eaters," for those so addled that they would even try to survive in such a place. "Rat-i-ron-taks" eventually became "Adirondacks," and became the name of a place future inhabitants would take great pride in. No longer does the term stand for a bunch of fools.

In time, the government of New York State proclaimed this area to be "a state park," but in truth it was a curious mixture of private and public holdings. When the twentieth century began a large portion of it was a major source of logs for lumber, and great hordes of lumberjacks roamed through the area, for the market for hemlock and pine and the various hardwoods expanded as the United States grew. There were large profits to be made on the backs of these legendary woodsmen.

Through certain areas of the Couchsacrage, great rivers run, making perfect highways to move the crop of logs. But in some places, "tote roads" were cut to enable teams of horses to draw wagonloads of the heavy harvest. In other places, crude railroad lines were built, and powerful little steam engines chugged along pulling and pushing flatcars loaded with logs to the sawmills.

Around the sawmills towns sprang up. The Couchsacrage, after all, could provide a cash crop for those strong enough to brave its challenges.

But as the century rolled on, things changed, the logs became less valuable, and at the same time, downstaters began to look at the Adirondacks more as a playground. Many who grew up in the wilderness, and loving it, turned from logging and other labors to guiding services to make a living. Even later, environmentalists declared that, instead of being a "dismal wilderness," the land was quite unique and remarkable, and for various reasons, began lobbying the state government to buy up and limit the use of large tracts of it, to the great consternation of the Adirondackers who had lived there for generations, and had staked their inherent claims to the land due to their long time presence and their gritty persistence.

In time, thousands of conterminous acres of swampland, dotted with hardwood islands, various glacial features, small ponds and brooks and stagnant pools, became property of the state, earmarked as "pristine wilderness," and allowed to vegetate back to its original condition.

Camps that had been leased by families for generations and generations had to be dismantled and deserted. Old men and women took one last look, tears running down their cheeks, as one precious memory after another raced through their consciousness. Then haltingly they drove away, to leave the Couchsacrage forever, down a road that would soon be closed and abandoned, and as they drove out of their precious corner of this wilderness they recalled vacations, and fishing and hunting with their closest friends, and great-grandparents and grandparents and parents and aunts and uncles, family members through to the present small children, who had filled the rustic edifice with joy and pleasure and laughter for years and years. It was all over now, and era had ended, time had passed them by. Like Mohecans and Arcadians, their likes would never be seen again.

With the roads gone, snowmobile trails were closed. Inns and motels and restaurants along the highway were closed too, for the seasonal customers no longer came. State highways through the Couchsacrage now winded through tunnels of trees and roadcuts, with abandoned and rotting and collapsing buildings along the way. Traffic dwindled, because small towns along the route diminished, no longer able to hold the younger generation, who had to move to find a livelihood.

The Couchsacrage was technically open to backpackers, sightseers, hunters, and fishermen who were willing to walk many miles for a small reward. In the Couchsacrage there was not much in terms of scenery, except for birds and trees and swamps and eskers and erratics. As the unmoderated vegetation took over, there was less and less available food for larger wildlife, so deer and bear and predators such as coyotes moved elsewhere. There wasn't much left in the Couchsacrage to sustain them.

Thus, the Couchsacrage became what it once was: a vast expanse of unused wilderness. Very few humans crossed through it, and those who did brought rations, lest they be reduced to "bark-eaters."

On this day, smack dab in the middle of it all, lay a small, one-engine, private airplane, crumpled against the side of a rugged hill, along the edge of a deep, thick, watery swamp. No one could see it, for visibility from any direction, aloft or otherwise, would be impossible. The grayness of a great ice storm had settled in, and a fine mist and gathering sleet had begun to settle about the little craft.

And even if one could see they would wonder, as they looked at the pitiful wreckage, with its smashed-in nose and its detached left wing, could anybody be alive in there?

Chapter 1

It was an ice storm, a big one, perhaps even bigger than the one that hung over the northeast in 1998. It had closed in over the Couchsacrage and much of the area around it, bringing with it the darkness, the cold, the constant mist and freezing rain.

In the normal behavior of the atmosphere, warm air is near the surface, and, being lighter than the air above it, has a tendency to rise. Many times, as the air rises, the pressure within it decreases, since there is less air on top, and the molecules spread apart, and less collisions occur, causing the temperature to drop. If a dew point is reached in this way, water may condense around dust particles, and precipitation may occur. Rain, produced this way, falls through the warmer air below, striking the surface of the earth as part of the everyday, normal, hydrologic cycle.

Sometimes, though, an abnormality occurs. Somehow, for complicated reasons, frigid air wedges in underneath the warm air.

Like an invisible pancake, this very cold air spreads across the land, relatively heavy, unable to rise, or even move.

To make matters worse, converging fronts about the continent trap these masses, preventing their normal advancement from one place to another. Thus they remain in one place. Not even the warm air goes anywhere.

This time, as the rain falls, it cools to the freezing point as it reaches the ground, and ice forms on trees, on power lines, on roads and sidewalks and bridges, and on the roofs of buildings. The clouds hang low, like an ominous curtain, and in the so-called "daylight hours" a dismal, depressing grayness invades the land. Intermittent curtains of a chilly lacy mist wafts about the countryside, and visibility is seriously impaired.

At night there is a darkness unsurpassed, the human eye receiving no stimulation whatsoever. Without some aid from artificial light, a human will experience total blindness.

In the darkness one hears the neverending cacophony of the sagging and straining trees, as they groan agonizingly while they bend from the weight of the accumulating ice; and then there is a sharp cracking as branches rip from their trunks, and sometimes entire trees come thundering to the ground.

There is no safety in the dark forest, with all of this going on. Nor is there safety on the highway, as trees and branches knock down poles and power lines, and often the complete darkness is interrupted by the sparks as electricity jumps from one severed wire to another, creating yet another hazard.

Yet there is also the continuous, monotonous tinkling as ice crystals bounce off obstacles everywhere. Roads and walkways are covered with a slimy, icy film. One can hardly walk, except with a careful measured shuffle. Vehicles often can't be controlled, the tendency to slide too much. Because of the icy roads, the toppling trees, the broken power lines, travel across the land is foolhardy and dangerous, just about impossible.

If someone were in any kind of trouble, it might take days for anyone bringing aid to cut their way through. Entire villages lose power. Homes are left in complete darkness. Stores are closed, either by the lack of light or by a shortage of goods to sell. Service stations are unable to pump gasoline. People hunker down in the darkness of their homes for days and days. Unless they live in a town that can open up a shelter of some kind, there is no place they can go. If they have a wood stove, and fuel, and stores of food, and a source of light, they may be comfortable.

Heaven forbid that there may be an emergency. All avenues of rescue are lost for the duration.

Chapter 2

"Hello! Governor's aide Morris Buba talking.

"Yes! The Times, how are you? Yes, the governor is aware of the plane crash. Yes, the plane's instruments sent us the geographical coordinates of where it went down. Yes. The governor's daughter, Angela, was aboard. She was heading for the ceremonies in Quebec City, she was to be New York State's symbolic representative there...

"Three people: the pilot, Ron Marks, very highly thought of; and a fine young man, one of Governor Bartholemew's best bodyguards, Mike Howell...

"Well, they had just left from Buffalo, Miss Bartholemew goes to college there...

"Some mechanical malfunction, we gather...

"Rescue? There are problems, big ones. As you know, there is a serious weather problem going on all over this region. Nobody can fly any craft in there. No visibility at all. And we lost all radio contact as well, as soon as the plane went down...

"Where? This is real bad news. In the middle of the Couchsacrage. Yes, that huge wilderness area in the Adirondack Park. No roads, no access by any kind of vehicle. Yes, forever wild. Very few people ever go in there, even in the best of conditions...

"Even the highways are icing over, and there are trees and power lines down everywhere. Every little town is a dark, lonely, island.

"ATVs? Four-wheelers? Well, the governor is in a box there. He promised the environmentalists that there would never be any motorized vehicles allowed in there again, ever. A number of those groups have already called here. They intend to hold him to his promise...

"Their take is that his daughter is no different from anybody else's daughter.

"Anyway, it's a moot point. No ATV could find any decent road to travel in there anyway. The Forest Ranger headquarters tells us that it's all grown up in there. All the old roads are now covered with thick vegetation and downed trees. Plus many of the brooks cross the old roads now, due to beaver dams and culvert washouts.

"Yes. We'll be glad to fax you a map of the area, marking where the plane is, but at this point...

"About eighteen miles, if you could walk, unimpeded in a straight line. I really don't know if anyone could get to that plane on foot, even.

"No. We don't know the medical condition of anybody who was on the plane. Of course the governor is worried sick about his

5

daughter.   Wouldn't you be? No. I don't think he has the constitutional power to over-ride environmental laws, the legislature would have to meet and pass a law, of course that would take weeks, maybe months.

"The nearest and best entrance is near a town called Bunchberry. Not too many people live there at this time of the year, not any more. It used to be a thriving town, years ago…

"Of course it looks bigger on a map. Summer homes! Seasonal residents who are in New York City, or Connecticut, or someplace else right now. It's a long story…

"Luckily we have been able to get one New York State Police Officer and one Forest Ranger into Bunchberry. They are to try and organize some sort of rescue team and try to get to the plane.

"I don't know their names, yet. The rest of the team will have to come from whoever is available. I understand that they are going over the town's roster of year around residents right now.

"We don't want a media circus up there. The roads are closed anyway. We are equipping the rescue party with phones and radios, and we'll share any information we have. Remember, police officers and rangers may not be able to walk through the Couchsacrage any faster than anybody else, we'll have to be patient.

"If the storm lifts, we probably can do more. No, the prognosis is not good. They say this storm can last for several more days.

"Right. This is not good, not good at all. We can only hope for some kind of miracle, I guess."

Chapter 3

TELEVISION NEWS RELEASE

"This is Bernard Gordon, with an WGHZ bulletin:

"Word has been received that a plane carrying Governor Harry Bartholemew's daughter, Angela, has crashed within New York State's Adirondack Park, which, as you all are aware, is currently enveloped in the ice storm.

"Besides Miss Bartholemew, the plane carried her escort, Michael Howell, and the pilot, Ronald Marks, both of Albany.

"Radio contact with the plane has been severed, but we can show you on this map where the crash site is located.

"Because of the storm, and the wilderness nature of the area, as designated by the New York State Department of Conservation, rescue by any other means except by foot are currently impossible.

"Word is that a rescue operation is presently being organized in the little Adirondack village of Bunchberry, located here." He pointed at the spot on the map behind him.

Alden L. Dumas

"Details at this time are still sketchy," he added.

"More later. Please stay tuned."

Chapter 4

Once it had been a farmhouse, for a family that was barely able to eke out a living trying to grow crops in the meager Adirondack soil. Then, for awhile, other families had lived there, as the breadwinners commuted to various nearby places of employment. But as the economy of the area died, the dwelling eventually was abandoned, the land going to some relative in a far away place. The little house, with its adjoining barn, had been left to the mercy of the forces of nature.

It was back from the road, accessible via a long driveway, hidden within a small copse of poplars and spruces, as the forest once again was reclaiming the land.

The house had been fixed over, made habitable again, not by a typical family, but rather by racketeers, drug dealers using the winding and remote Adirondack roads to transport their merchandise from the border of Quebec to the large southern tier cities of New York State. Major highways such as U.S. 81 and U.S. 87 were simply too well patrolled by the police.

The nearest village to this small domicile was the tiny settlement of Eagle's Aerie, but the locals posed no threat to the gangsters, as the inhabitants of the area tended to mind their own business, and leave "outsiders" alone.

At this moment in time, three men were there, all of them drivers, all delivery boys. Clean cut Woody, with his straight back and broad shoulders, stood near the front window, staring at what little driveway he could see through the darkness of the storm. The others, a tall, scrawny, pimply punk named Pauly, and a short robust Russian immigrant called Vasily, were occupied in a room that once served previous owners as a dining area.

On the table were neat packages of cocaine and crack, and of marijuana, waiting to be distributed among the drivers to fill their various orders. There wasn't enough here, but another shipment was to arrive soon. That is, if the other driver could fight the storm well enough.

"Damned weather!" Woody exclaimed, his frustration showing. "You can hardly see anything at all!"

Pauly had done all the sorting he could do for now. "I wonder if Farley and Martinson are actually trying to travel today," he offered, as he awkwardly sprawled on the ragged remains of what used to be a sofa, and opened a can of beer.

"Well, at least the roads are just as bad for the cops," Vasily observed, relief in his voice. "Where I come from, police are always bad to see." His family had come to America to escape oppression.

"And that's what Cheese likes about these back roads," Woody reminded him, "The big highways are thick with cops, but you don't see too many back here."

"Except for those damned trainees," Pauly observed, "jeezus, they're like boy scouts after a merit badge."

"Yeah! But they'd rather harass some poor working stiff who's had four beers on his way home from work. Easier pickins," Woody commented, as he watched Pauly finish his brew and reach for another can. "By the way, Pauly, haven't you had enough? We're going to run out."

"It looks like we're almost out," Pauly observed sadly.

"Well, Farley and Martinson always bring some good Canadian stuff when they come," Vasily reminded him.

"Yeah, if they get here," Pauly said.

"Here comes somebody," Woody interrupted, still gazing at the dark driveway. He noticed the late model Jaguar. "It's Vitilli."

"Vitilli?" Vasily remarked, "He's not due today. What's Cheese up to? Is he checking up on us?"

"There's a lot of money tangled up in our deals this month," Woody reminded him.

"Maybe they think we'll sort of line our own pockets," Pauly put in. The thought had crossed his mind more than once.

"I wouldn't dare," Vasily replied. "These are vicious people, and they would hunt you down. There would be no escape."

11

Woody shuddered. That was the problem, as he had lately become aware of. This whole operation was far bigger than he had bargained for when he had naively signed on for some extra money, months before. Now he was having second thoughts. He wanted to get out of this business altogether, but there might not be any avenue available to do so. He was now potentially a witness, and all witnesses were earmarked to die. It was Cheese's first directive.

By now three men were entering the door. The first was short, dark, swarthy. It was Bo Vitilli, who was responsible for the drug distribution business in this particular neck of the woods. He was temperamental and mean-spirited. No one dared to cross him.

Next were his two executioners, two men as different from one another as any two men of the same occupation could be.

Vitilli's right hand man, his first lieutenant so to speak, was Mac MacIlwaine: tall, erudite, gentlemanly. He had the appearance of a learned man, a college professor. Many men were now dead because they were totally caught off balance by his cold earnest blue eyes.

Abdul was also tall. He was dark complected, with piercing eyes, eyes so dark that a pupil was undetectable. His face was expressionless, like the countenance on an evil statue. He rarely talked, and often appeared to be staring off at another world someplace. But there was no doubt that he was the one feared the most by the others.

"Whew!" Woody thought. "Cheese has sent the first-team!"

It was Vitilli who spoke first. "Cheese sent me to warn you," he glared, "some snitch somewhere has pointed out this cabin…"

"Oh no!" It was Vasily. His experiences around Grozny, in the old country, led him to believe that trouble would be manifesting very soon.

"We have some barrels buried in the woods behind here," Vitilli went on. "We're going to have to stash the stuff until later, when things cool down. If it really gets hot around here, we are to clear out, and this little bungalow might get hit by lightning."

"We may have to clear out in clean cars," MacIlwaine added, matter-of-factly.

"What about the drugs?" Pauly asked.

"Cheese's problem for now," Vitilli answered. "He'll get the stuff back sometime, when the time is right."

"We're still waiting for Martinson and Farley," Vasily reported. "They are due any minute now."

Vitilli sighed. "I was afraid of that," he said anxiously, "and they have a shipment of drugs in their car, don't they?"

"The roads are terrible!" MacIlwaine reported. "We just barely got through. We spun out a few times, and tree branches are reaching across the road, power lines are sagging…"

"It's hell out there," Vitilli agreed. "Even Abdul was scared."

The dark man in the corner just stared blankly, not acknowledging Vitilli's comment at all. Some of the other men suppressed quiet chuckles.

MacIlwaine had his pistol out now, and was checking the load. Abdul followed suit, as did Vitilli.

The other three men did not carry handguns. Vitilli could see the confused look on their faces.

"When Martinson's Saturn comes up the drive way, "He said menacingly, "they'd better be alone!"

Chapter 5

By highway, it was exactly thirty-eight miles from Eagle's Aerie to Bunchberry, though both were located along the perimeter of The Couchsacrage.

In a different cabin off of the road, another group of men were also riding out the storm.

This so-called "camp" was actually an old mobile home, moved from the old Bunchberry Trailer Park, and now stationed just off the main road, on a few acres still privately owned by a local character called Fat Frank. "The state ain't found it yet!" he often exclaimed.

Fat Frank and his buddies once belonged to a well maintained lodge back many miles into the Couchsacrage, but once the state had purchased the land from their leasers, they'd had to destroy their beloved camp and move out. To a man they were still very bitter about the whole sequence of events.

But today was kind of a good day. They had a nice wood fire going, and they had several propane lights burning. On the porch was a cooler of beer, and four men were hunched over the card table. It was a perfect way to ride out the storm.

The darkening shadow of a large building could be seen across the street.

"The lights are out over to the Pig's Head Tavern," Poley East observed. He bent down to adjust the position of his left leg, which was in a cast.

"Old Harvey will be firing up the generator soon," he added.

"That is if Harvey remembered to stock up on gasoline," Ramsey chuckled, "you know how Harvey is!"

The men had already enjoyed a good laugh. Ramsey had bid a "hozzy" without possessing the right bower. The others had looked upon this futile effort with disbelief. Apparently the veteran player had been overcome with an excess of zeal, or had been under the influence of "too many suds," as Dag had explained.

"That'll cost you ten points, and you owe each of us a dollar!" Poley, the scorekeeper declared. "Who got that other point? Oh yeah, Frank did."

Back when their lodge had been in existence, hozzie points were worth a quarter, but they had decided to up the ante in recent years.

"What the hell were you thinking?" Fat Frank was asking. Fat Frank was considered to be the best player, and such a move was incomprehensible. It was his turn to deal, and he grinned as he went about his business. The pile of dollar bills in front of him indicated that he was having a good day indeed.

Joe "Dag" Dagonneault stretched. He looked outside as the storm continued as the light gradually diminished. "This is almost like the old days," he remarked, "although no place in existence today is like the old camp we had in the Couchsacrage." Then, with a large sigh of regret, he added, "Dirty state land grabbing bastards!"

All along the fringe of the Couchsacrage there were many people who felt as he did.

"Are there any jacks in that deck?" he grumbled, "My job seems to be to sit here and throw out cards so you other guys can play! I pass, again!"

"Would you like some cheese with that whine?" Poley, snickered. "Three is my bid."

"Damn you, East," Ramsey cried. "I was gonna bid three!"

"Four!" Fat Frank announced emphatically.

"You overbid me all the time!" Poley exclaimed, his voice tinged with exasperation.

"It's Poley's turn to whine," Dag reminded everyone.

The hand went quickly, with Frank taking the first four tricks. Ramsey eagerly grabbed up the last. "Now I'm only nine in the hole" he announced.

Poley grabbed his pencil and marked on the score pad in front of him. Dag reached for the cards, a halo of smoke encircling his head from the little cigar he was puffing on.

Suddenly, they were interrupted by a knock on the door.

"Who the hell would be out in this weather?" mumbled Frank, as he headed for the door.

"Must be Harvey needs gas," Poley joked.

As the door swung open, a smallish, short figure stepped inside. It was a New York State Police Officer, a woman. She was in full uniform, and the rain was dripping from her hat.

"Hi, Rose!" each man said in unison. They all knew her. She had recently been assigned to the Bunchberry area, but she had made it her mission to meet as many local people as she could. As far as she could see at the time, she had drawn an easy assignment. In her initial assessment of the local citizenry, she had concluded that there was nobody in the village of Bunchberry that wasn't a down-to-earth law-abiding citizen.

"Can I come in?" she asked.

"Of course, of course!" all four men exclaimed, in unison once again.

Most of the new troopers to the area were young, green, inexperienced. Rose seemed to be different, somehow. She didn't look as young as the other officers, and she carried herself with an enigmatic air of confidence.

Every man who sat at the table respected her. She seemed to be above the rest in her ability to balance compassion and fairness with her duties to enforce the law. To the small town Adirondacker, this was a trait to be admired.

"You look like you're on duty," Frank noted, "or we would offer you a beer."

"A soda would be nice," she answered, noting from the looks of the men at the table that that request would probably not be able to be filled.

"I'm here on business," she went on. "I need to talk to all of you, particularly Dag."

Poley looked disappointed. "It's not because he's the best looking, that's for sure."

Rose laughed. "No, it's because he's the healthiest specimen among you. If you hadn't broken your leg last month, Poley, I would be looking for you."

"Besides, if it's official business, you might not want to go," Fat Frank added, looking at Poley. Poley, the bachelor, certainly would have welcomed a chance to spend time with the pretty policewoman.

"I don't think he would," Rose agreed, thinking of her mission. This was not a social occasion.

"An accident?" Dag was asking.

"You could say that," Rose answered, "but it's nobody you know. Nobody from around here."

Each of the four men looked at her intently, curiosity in their eyes.

"Didn't you once have a camp deep in the Couchsacrage?" she asked. "I was told that you did."

Dag fought back the urge to utter an expletive. But Rose Fernandez was not to blame for what had come to pass. "Years ago," he answered softly.

"I was told that you had held that lease for a long long time," she went on.

"For generations," Dag said. "We all knew the land like the back of our hands."

"I could still get around in there," Poley added, "probably even at night without a light."

"That's why I'm here," Rose nodded. "Dag, how long ago was the last time you were in there?"

"Not for a while," Dag answered, this time the hint of anger building up. "How the hell <u>can</u> you get in there? The roads are gone, either grown up with plants or crossed by blow-down. Many of the culverts have washed away, and the various brooks now are washing away the old road. Some places are inundated by beaver ponds, although with good boots you might be able to cross some of these places. Nevertheless, it's quite a walk for nothing. That's why nobody, and I mean nobody, goes in there anymore."

"There was a foot trail," Rose mentioned.

"But there's nothing to see!" Dag exclaimed. "It's flat, no scenic vistas. Years ago, when the D.E.C. had budget problems, they let it all go to seed."

"I hope all those New York City politicians got their money's worth," Ramsey commented. They all nodded, even though they thought Rose might be from the city herself.

"Some of us are in poor health," Frank added. "In the old days we could have driven in there and still enjoyed the place. My grandfather did until the day he died. My dad did even when he was over eighty years old. Now nobody enjoys it. What do I pay taxes for?"

"All gone now," Ramsey said sadly, shaking his head.

"I need somebody to take me in there," Rose remarked. She could feel the bitterness in their voices, and she felt sympathy for her friends' resentfulness. But she had a job to do.

"Well, the next time my son is up for a visit..." Dag began to offer.

"No. I mean tomorrow morning. Early."

Poley chuckled. "A case of back country rescue," he chuckled. He rubbed his lucky broken leg. "Yup. Dag's your man all right!"

The others caught on immediately, and agreed with Poley.

"Dag always knew the land better than the rest of us," Fat Frank winked. Others were quick to join in with comments about Dag's abilities as a backcountry guide.

Dag's face reddened as he absorbed the barbs from his comrades.

"There's a plane crash near where your camp used to be," Rose went on, ignoring the jocularity. "The governor's daughter was aboard. They have not made any radio contact, and we have to go in there..."

21

"The governor's daughter?" Ramsey asked, unbelievingly.

Rose looked sad. She looked tired. "The storm will go on," she said, "and the nearest and best access to the wreck site is right here in Bunchberry. And I'm the only trooper available at this point."

"You need somebody younger than me!" Dag protested.

Rose looked at him impatiently. "Who can I get to go here in Bunchberry? You are the only person available in this village who can do what we need. If you can suggest somebody within walking distance who can guide us on that property who has more knowledge than you, I'll go and get him, and I'll leave you be."

She was right. They all knew it. Dag was the best man available.

"Who else can go?" Dag said, with resignation. This had to be some sort of bad dream.

"D.E.C. Forest Ranger Pete Randolph," she answered.

Dag's nostrils flared. "I don't want to go anywhere with that stiff, pompous, know-it-all tree-hugger."

"But you'll go as a favor to me?" Rose asked, showing him a beautiful smile.

"Who could resist," he cracked playfully, but with some irony in his voice.

Chapter 6

In a small three-room bungalow in downtown Bunchberry, Henry "Doc" Ginsberg reached for his bottle of scotch one more time. He drank too much, and he knew it, but he didn't care.

He had lit one small candle, lest he sit in total blackness. Yet the cheery dancing light did little to sooth his state of despair.

The tiny flicker caused shadows, causing each bit of furniture in the room to create a lurking dark hulk, an ominous creature to witness what he perceived himself to be, the pitiful soul at the table.

"The worst part is that I'll feel even worse in the morning," he told himself, aloud, as if there was somebody else in the house. He was well experienced in these lonesome-drinking bouts. He wished he could resist, to toss the drink aside, to go on without it. On one shoulder was a voice that said, "This is wrong, throw the booze away." But the stronger voice on the other shoulder said, "One more drink will make things easier to take. Nobody cares anyhow."

In his half stupor he was still in Africa. The rebels were invading the village. He was attending to his friend, Caleb, who was suffering from an abdominal bullet wound. Caleb could survive, if proper care was forthcoming, but there was no time. Transport was impossible, and he, Doc Ginsberg was alone. The rebels were entering town at that very moment.

The drink was gone, and Doc reached once more for the bottle to slake his thirst. "God help me!" he cried.

His memory lapsed back to the African village once again. The rebels! They were not kind to prisoners. Torture and slow death was their common practice. Anyone would be fair game: women, children, wounded, they were all the same.

As Doc thought back to those days he trembled. The scotch ran down his throat like some soothing tonic. If only he could forget!

He had run. The rebels were too close. He had deserted his friend and ran. As he reached the hills on the outskirts of town he had heard the screams from below. Screams of his friend, Caleb, as the rebels demanded information.

The screams continued to rattle through Henry Ginsberg's mind, after all these years. "If only they would go away!" he cried again and again.

The tears flowed down his face again, and his hand trembled as he poured another drink. "If I had stayed," he sobbed, regretfully, "I would be dead, but I would not suffer as I have suffered."

The screams continued in his ears. He put his head down on the table, and tried to rest. "It really won't do any good," he told himself, "Every night is worse than the night before."

He had moved from his home in Ithaca to this quiet town in the Adirondacks, to get away from it all. The change of scenery might help, as his psychiatrist friend had advised him. But matters had gotten all the worse. There simply was more quiet time to think.

"If only I had the guts to end it all!" he scolded himself. He was even too much of a coward to commit suicide. "What kind of poor creature am I?" he asked himself. The disgust in his voice echoed through the small, lonely cabin.

For a time he listened to the pelting rain on the roof, then he hung his head, and passed out, with no comprehension of the world about him.

Then it seemed someone was banging on the door, and shouting his name.

"Doc! You in there?" the voice asked.

Drunkenly Doc rose to his feet, and stumbled to the door. Another person to talk to would delay his pain. Anybody's company was welcome indeed.

Forest Ranger Pete Randolph was already letting himself in. "How's the old renaissance man tonight?" he asked. All over town Doc Ginsberg was known as a well- educated man of many talents.

Doc smiled stupidly. "Not too good tonight, sir."

25

Pete was a man who did not make "small talk." He was known for his impersonal businesslike demeanor. "I was told that you have some medical training," he blurted.

"Oh, God!" Doc cried. The screams again! If only he could be free!

Pete ignored the drunken man's apparent anguish. "Well? It says on my computer read out that you were a medical student at Cornell, and that you still have E.M.T. certification…"

Doc reached for his glass again. "It still haunts me!" he whispered. It was a response that made no sense to the Forest Ranger at all.

"We need your help," the ranger went on indifferently. "There's been a plane crash. Maybe serious casualties, deep in the woods. You are one of the few who can help us, due to the ice storm and all…"

"I can't go! I'm not good enough. I'm worthless. Leave me alone!" Doc cried.

Pete showed no sympathy. His voice expressionless, drab, unfeeling. "Nonsense. You're drunk and I need you sober by early morning. You are to come downtown with me right now, and leave your booze behind. If you don't willingly go with me now, I will have to arrest you and take you anyway, even if I have to go for help first."

Doc looked at him in disbelief.

"I'll get you up bright and early to pack your medical things," Pete went on, "and we'll provide what you don't have. Be prepared for broken bones, open wounds, and trauma."

"We might need blood!" Doc cried. The description of the possible wounds had awakened a certain part of him.

"We can only do what we can do," Pete said bluntly, "No more, no less. You are to come with me now."

Chapter 7

The roads around Eagle's Aerie are crooked and narrow, and with the visibility considerably limited by the storm, the two young New York State Police officers knew that they had been given a difficult task.

"Look for a light green '07 Saturn SL," Officer Don Jones reminded his partner, Luke Williams. Their car was parked in an ancient driveway, and it was hidden behind a thick balsam fir, adding another impediment to their ability to see. "The brass is closing in on the drug trafficking ring, and they think that this car might be carrying some interesting cargo."

"Yeah, I heard," Luke replied, lazily. "They think that there might be a hideout near here somewhere."

"Can you imagine?" Don could hardly conceal his enthusiasm. "What a big chance for us."

Luke was nowhere near as gung-ho. "Could be dangerous," he answered. "I'd like to live long enough to collect my pension." He and Don had just recently finished their training, and it seemed to him that this assignment might just be a little bit over their heads. He felt more than a little nervous. This was a little bigger than chasing down a drunk driver or a speeder.

Don did not share his apprehension. "It's the storm!" he stated, "the big shots can't get here. They're leaving it all up to us."

They had been sitting by the highway for hours now, and their comfort level was diminishing. To run the motor was to risk detection, although both doubted that, due to the icy roads, any driver noticing them would be able to turn and make any sort of getaway. Still, as vigilantly as they could, they would be careful. Ice was building up everywhere, including on their troop car, and as Don sat by the wheel, Luke often found himself out in the elements, scraping windows.

The clouds were hanging very close to the ground, forming opaque and translucent curtains that regularly changed their shapes.

"The weather report calls for a long spell of this stuff," Don was saying, "this storm could be something."

Officer Luke Williams was thinking of his wife, Ann, and their baby, little Trevor. Already it looked like the weather would prevent him from being home soon, maybe not for several days. "The worst part of this job," he thought, "are days like this."

Don Jones was already anticipating another sort of adventure. "Did I tell you? I've got tickets for the big Notre Dame-Syracuse showdown at the Carrier Dome next Saturday. Good seats too! And

I'm going over to a buddy's fraternity after the game for a big party. A lot of beautiful co-eds will be there!"

Luke couldn't help but smile. He remembered the years before he had met Ann, but to him those bachelor days had been sort of a lonely existence. But Jonesy was more suited for that sort of life. In fact, Jonesy was the type who might never get married at all. He was having too good a time. Luke closed his eyes and saw the face of his little son. "I sure miss that kid," he thought.

They sat in silence for about thirty minutes. Stake out work involved a lot of intervals like that. Most of what was being received over the radio scanner was static, interrupted by far away messages to go to the aid of one party or another. But where Don and Luke were stationed, not much was going on due to the bad weather, especially in their neck of the woods.

Headlights! Hey! There was a car coming up the road, and it seemed to be going just a little too fast for the road conditions. They looked carefully through the grayish haze. A light green Saturn flashed by.

"That's it," Luke said. "Let's go!"

Don started the motor and flicked on the flashers. The police car spun its wheels slightly as they tried to turn up the main highway. When they made the turn, the greasy road caused the car to swerve wildly to the left, and they almost skidded off the road.

"Holy cow," Don said, as his hands flew around the steering wheel, righting the course of the car. "Pursuit will not be easy on these roads."

Chapter 8

Bo Vitilli was a temperamental and vile man. Nobody liked him, and almost everybody feared him. He was unforgiving and zealous in his quest for vengeance when he believed that he had been double crossed. His penchant for cruel violence was well known.

He paced about the cabin, his pupil-less dark eyes piercing everybody he looked at.

"Where the hell are Martinson and Farley?" he worried, staring out the window. The two drug runners were late for their rendezvous, and it was getting dark mighty fast.

In his mind he tried to assess the men in the room. If there was going to be a problem because of the storm, he wanted to be sure of who could be counted on.

MacIlwaine and he had been through a lot. He was pure gold.

Abdul was a strange one. A lot of secrets there. Somebody had told him that a lot of Abdul's money went toward a cause in

Afghanistan to overthrow the U.S. government. Vitilli shrugged. "A man with a cause can be very reliable," he thought.

Vasily was a follower. No trouble with the Russian.

Pauly was dangerous. A cocky crack addict whose behavior was very unpredictable. "All of his bad habits might just kill that boy," Vitilli thought, "then again, I might even have to kill him myself."

Woody was the mystery. Most of the rest were city thugs, but he was a country boy. The breed was unfamiliar to Vitilli. Woody could stand some watching.

Then there was the missing two.

Martinson seemed to have a continuous smirk on his face, like he knew a secret that he would not tell you; but Martinson was a man of many talents, and Vitilli knew that if he needed another enforcer, another man to kill for him, Martinson was the man he could use.

The other guy, Farley, as far as Vitilli was concerned, was a jerk. He was high strung and nervous and his general temperament made Vitilli nervous. Still, the short, stocky lad had been a reliable employee.

"Where are those guys?" Vitilli worried once again.

The dismal storm weighed on everybody's mind, and Vitilli became more and more convinced that everyone should just lie low. It would do no one any good for one of their delivery cars to crash and the contents be discovered.

Suddenly, his portable phone rang. He clicked it on.

"Curly's," he said. It was code talk, in case someone outside was monitoring the call.

"What's for dinner?" It was Martinson's voice. He was calling from his car phone and Vitilli didn't like the message. Martinson was warning Vitilli that the cops were on his tail, and needed permission to "come home."

"Spaghetti," Vitilli replied.

"My favorite!" This meant that there was no chance to lose the pursuers. Martinson would be coming up the driveway.

"Okay, son," Vitilli hissed, "how long?"

"Fifteen minutes, maybe. The roads are terrible! Let's hope we don't get blocked by a tree or a power line."

Vitilli hung up the phone. Martinson and Farley were in a box.

This was the worst possible picture. He had been warned that the cops had been informed of Cheese's operation, and they were closing in. He had already made plans to move the whole operation to another location. They were now out of time.

The only escape left for Martinson and Farley was right up that driveway outside. "We might have to kill some cops," he declared. "Let's hope that, in this weather, there will be only one car, with no chance of support."

He turned to the men. "Hide all the cars. Back behind the barn, or behind the hill near it. Be quick."

This part had been rehearsed. With unwanted visitors on the way, make the cabin look deserted. Maybe the trouble would blow by.

All of the drivers hustled outside, buttoning their coats as they went.

"It seems kind of silly," Woody thought, as he pulled his pick-up behind the barn. "In this soupy weather, nobody can see the house from the highway anyhow."

Vitilli, MacIlwaine and Abdul were checking their pistols. They were Cheese's militia, his enforcers, his hired guns.

Vitilli was full of worry. Nobody was going to trap him, no sir! As he strained his eyes peering down the almost totally black driveway, he knew he would do what he could to protect the organization, and their way of doing business.

There better be only one set of headlights coming up that hill! There better not be a police car. No sir. There better not be.

Chapter 9

Miles away, another New York State police car moved slowly down through what once had been the main street of Bunchberry. The rain, the sleet, the icy roads and the poor visibility all were cause for Officer Rose Fernandez's caution.

By her side was Dag Dagonneault. She had convinced him to leave the card game at Fat Frank's camp, and allow her to drive him home.

"We're going to try and get a few hours sleep," she told him. "But we'll be up early. We'll try to be in the Couchsacrage before dawn."

Dag had been quite silent since leaving the camp. He seemed to be in a thoughtful mood.

"So many houses, so few residents. No wonder we can't find anyone to help," she commented. She spoke partly to herself, but her voice was loud enough for her to see if any of it would get a reaction from Dag.

"It wasn't always this way," he responded. "This was once a thriving community, all year round. We had a lumber mill, a box factory, shops, even our own dairy. There were children, a school. I graduated from here."

"What happened?" Rose asked. She was from a long way away. All of this emptiness was very foreign to her.

"Well," Dag retorted, "the state bought the land around here. Nobody was allowed to cut the trees any more. The lumber mill closed, and the box factory closed. Men were out of work all over the place."

"But that was long ago," she replied.

"Yes, and the town formed a planning committee to try and find something that people could do to turn the economy around again. We tried to retool the old factory to make clothes, but various outside busybodies objected. Do you realize how many carpetbaggers there are in and around the Adirondacks? Practically none of these people grew up here, but they don't mind running our business."

Dag continued, "We even had a chance to build a prison on the old mill site. We thought that that would be environmentally compatible.

"We even had the government in Albany on our side on that one, but you know what? A national environmental organization stepped in. Most of their members don't even live in this state, and probably never even visited here. They said that they would tie up the whole project in court, holding it up for years, and they had the money to do it. So we were left high and dry.

"People left town. No work.

"That's about it. Then it got worse. Old Norm Calloway sold his old rickety house to some city slicker for a bundle. They wanted to make a summer cottage out of it. Now, everybody put 'for sale' signs on their lots. Local people, especially with growing families, could not afford the prices. The rich from downstate and other places moved in for the summer, and our young people moved out. Thus the death of Bunchberry."

"In the summer it's a boom town," Rose said. "I've been here."

"The final straw was when we had to close our school," Dag said sadly. "We really lost our identity then."

Rose sighed. "I guess a lot of Adirondack villages can say the same. Many are ghost towns in the winter now. But at least somebody is still here in Bunchberry."

"Yep. Us caretakers!" Dag said bitterly, referring to the new common job of watching over the summer people's homes.

"You haven't sold your home," she noted.

"It belongs to my son, Dave. I hope he sells it for a bundle and moves to Tahiti," Dag responded angrily. He had come to realize that the root of his indignation was now a lost cause.

By now the car had pulled up to his front door. Rose was thankful that she had been driving so slowly. Stopping on the greasy road was very difficult, and the vehicle skidded for several feet before it came to a rest.

She looked out in the direction of Dag's cottage, but in the weather and the enveloping darkness, it was very difficult to see, in spite of the glow from the car's headlights.

"I'll bet Dave keeps it," Rose declared.

"For a summer home," Dag agreed, a large dose of sadness in his voice. He and his kind had lived and died on the land that they loved for generations, but they had been out voted, out spent, and had been overwhelmed by the politics of the times. Legislators from metropolitan areas could care less about the feelings of a few thousand Adirondackers.

He was a tired and bitter man.

"It's really dark in there," Rose was saying. "Do you live alone?"

"My wife died years ago. It was hard on her too, to see the town die like that."

Rose turned her spotlight on the front steps. "Need a flashlight?" she asked.

"Thanks," he smiled. "I've got one by the door, once I'm inside."

"Better get some rest," she smiled. "We meet at the town hall at 4:30."

Dag chuckled. "The 'town hall,' as if there was a town," he thought.

"If you're not there I'll come and get you," she said sweetly. But she meant what she said.

"Gotcha!" he answered, mocking fear. Then he scratched his bewhiskered chin. "I want you to know that I don't mind helping you," he said, "You seem to be a caring and professional person. There are people's lives at stake, I know. And you've got a job to do."

"It will be hard for you to cross old familiar lands again," she said, thoughtfully, "both physically and emotionally. There will be a lot of old memories."

"Well, I'm still mad as hell that the property ended up the way it did," he declared as he opened up the car door.

She reached over and grabbed his shoulder. "Where is your son now?" she asked.

"He tried to stay," he answered. "But he's a school teacher, and there is no work for him here."

She kept a light on him as he moved up onto his porch and through the front door, which she noticed he did not keep locked. Being from the city she shook her head. This would have been very foolhardy where she came from.

In a moment she could see the beam of a flashlight from the inside.

The electrical power in the town had been out for quite some time now, but with the headlights she could see the steady flow of ice pellets as they swirled through the beam of light to affix themselves on any and all solid surfaces.

She thought of the footing in the Couchsacrage, and shook her head as she drove off.

Chapter 10

There is a little brook that runs through a small part of the Couchsacrage called Chub Pond Creek, so called because it serves as an outlet for Chub Pond, a small water filled kettle a mile or so to the north. In summer, this little stream often nearly dries up, and it rarely ever amounts to much, since the marshland it crosses, Polecat Swamp, sponges up a good deal of the moisture anyway. Only when it is dammed up by beavers, or when a substantial amount of precipitation falls, does it ever hold or carry much water.

One could say that Chub Pond Creek is about as insignificant a stream as there was anywhere in America, and it only had a name because loggers and hunters once occupied the area along its banks.

There is a small rocky outcrop of metamorphic rock that borders the west side of the creek, and it also is insignificant, as far as any large picture of the area might indicate. Loggers and hunters had given this relatively high ground a name also: Baldy Peak Hill.

But fate had intervened, and in an instant had made each a landmark that would play a major role in our story. For on this misty, dark, cold and icy day, a small, one engine private plane had descended rapidly, and had passed just a yard or two above the brook, and as it broke through branches of the various species of trees that were along its banks, had crashed hard against Baldy Peak Hill.

From above, due to the thickness of the cloud cover, and later as the twilight succumbed to darkness, not even a hawk or a raven could see down upon it. It was a quiet, lonely, pitiful sight, with its left wing torn off, and its nose bashed in to the side of the hill. Already the outside of the fuselage was covered by a thick onionskin of ice. And more was to come, much more, as the relentless dripping from the sky above continued.

Just before the crash had occurred, the pilot, Ron Marks, had sent his last futile message to the outside world. Other equipment had provided the exact longitude and latitude of the craft just before all signals stopped.

All instruments were dead now. Like some long lost craft on a distant planet, the cold wreckage lay bent and crooked in the impending darkness.

All had been still now for hours. Only the steady dripping of the freezing rain broke the silence.

Chapter 11

Back at the farm-house in Eagle's Aerie, Vitilli had chosen to sit in the darkness. The power had been off for some time anyway, and even though there was a supply of flashlights and lanterns, he and MacIlwaine had chosen to keep a dark and intense vigil as they stared through the window and out at the driveway.

He wanted the illusion that no one occupied the house. He had ordered all lights turned off.

"You guys lay low," he had commanded the others. "if we get unwanted company, the less they know, the better."

By now everybody sat in silence. Each felt an uneasiness. Trouble was pending.

Then they saw the headlights. A car was heading toward the cabin.

"That better be our boys," Vitilli hissed.

The car's lights went off. But there was no darkness. An eerie glow indicated that another car was heading up the driveway as well, and this one had red flashing dome lights. Already, Martinson and Farley had jumped out of their car.

Vitilli, MacIlwaine and Abdul were out in the yard in a flash. "Close the damn door!" Vitilli said as he left, "and for chrissakes, be quiet!"

In the darkness, they could hear Farley's panicky whine. "What'll we do? What'll we do?"

"Calm down!" Vitilli ordered with a loud whisper. "Act natural. We'll be about, here in the darkness. And let Martinson do the talking."

As far as Vitilli was concerned, Farley was way too high strung. The key here was to keep the cops from snooping around. Nobody should do anything that looked suspicious. Martinson was more likely to be cool in a situation like this.

Farley licked his lips nervously. He had noticed the pistol in Vitilli's hand as he slipped away in the gloom.

By now the police car had pulled up behind Martinson's Saturn. The door opened, and a lone officer emerged.

"Hello, there!" Officer Don Jones was saying. "Can I see your license and registration, please?"

So far it was a normal stop. Nothing to be concerned about.

"I sure hope I wasn't speeding," Martinson said jovially, as he handed his credentials to the policeman. "That would be pretty dangerous in weather like this."

Officer Jones was to the point. "Actually we've been on the look out for a car like yours. We'd like you and your partner there to put your hands up on the cab."

The other officer stood up beside the police car, and they could see he was holding a revolver, just to be on the safe side.

Martinson and Farley did as they were told. This situation was deteriorating rapidly.

"What's going on?" Farley asked, trying his most innocent tone.

"I'm afraid we're going to have to search your car," the officer was now saying. This was not what they wanted to happen at all.

"Why?" Martinson demanded. "What's going on?"

"No need to be concerned," the officer was saying. "Kind of routine out here in the middle of nowhere."

"I doubt that you search every car," Farley said, his innocent tone gone.

By now the policeman was inside the Saturn, shining his flashlight to and fro. Martinson and Farley looked with fear at the other officer, Luke Williams, as he menacingly held his gun on them.

Officer Jones had already emerged from the vehicle. He was holding some objects in his hand, and there was no doubt what they were. He held them up so that his partner could see.

The officer by the car was speaking now. "I'm afraid you will both have to come with us. We found what we were looking for, and…"

He never finished his sentence. Flames of gunfire erupted from the nearby bushes. The noise was deafening, the fight totally one sided. Each police officer screamed, and lurched in pain, and then died in the snow.

Farley grabbed one of the flashlights, and watched with morbid fascination as the blood flowed out on the ice.

"What are we going to do now?" he asked, panic gripping his voice.

Chapter 12

Fear! Paralyzing, indescribable fear! Fear so intense that normal contact with the environment is tempered, compromised, and surreal.

Angela Bartholemew, daughter of the governor of the great state of New York, was coming to.

She was blind. She knew that. With her eyes wide open, she could see nothing at all.

Also, there was the constant throbbing of a pain in her head. She was still strapped in to her airplane seat, and she wasn't sure she should try to move at all.

Memory began to flash back. It had happened so quickly. Pilot Ron Marks had been cursing the storm. Visibility had been zero. The plane, obviously, had lost altitude for some reason, and suddenly there had been trees, way too close, and then the plane lurched as it hit branches. Someone had screamed, perhaps it had been her. But then everything had turned black. It was hard to tell how long she had been out cold.

Now there was the blindness, and the head pain.

Fear of the unknown now gripped her. She had a sudden brief wish that she had died quickly, it would have been better than a slow death within the wreck of the plane.

Still, she could hear. That was good news. Rain or hail or something was pelting the outside of the fuselage.

She sensed that the pain in her head was lessening, and she reached up to touch her forehead. First she felt the stickiness of what she assumed was blood, and then the gash itself. She quickly withdrew her hand. Perhaps it was this wound that had caused her to lose her sight.

Angela, though, was at heart a fighter. If there was anything she could do to help herself, she would get on with it.

"C'mon, girl," she scolded herself, "Get a grip! You only need to survive until help comes." She fought hard to overcome the feelings of terror that wanted to overwhelm her.

She breathed deeply, and tried to find something positive to think about. The instincts for survival began to emerge.

She fumbled at the buckles that held her seat belts, and slowly, as she freed herself, she was relieved to find that her joints and limbs seemed to be lame, but everything seemed to move all right. There was no other severe pain except for her head.

She also sensed a severe chill, and a slight moist breeze that flowed from in front of her. Now that she had awakened, she was cold.

Alden L. Dumas

There were two other passengers on the plane, the pilot, and a young man who had been assigned the job as her bodyguard.

"Mike," she called to him, haltingly, worried about what she might find.

No answer.

"Mike!" This time her voice was more like a scream.

No answer.

Carefully she slid from her seat, and crept to where her escort, Mike Howell, might be still stationed. Gently she shook him, whispering his voice as she did.

He groaned.

The sound was a relief to her. At least she wasn't alone. "Thank God!" she exclaimed.

"Miss Bartholemew?" he asked softly, with a sight gurgling voice.

The feebleness of his voice threw her. It was not what she had expected from the strong, virile young man.

"Yes, it's me," she said, trying to sound comforting.

"What a relief," he answered, sounding better, "I've been awake several times, but you didn't respond."

"I'm sorry. I just came to. We've been in quite a crash," she said, stating the obvious. "Are you all right?"

"I don't think so," he answered evenly, as if trying to control emotions. "I can't move my legs. They are numb. No feeling there."

50

"Oh Lord," she responded anxiously. "I may be blind. I took a bad blow to my head." The dread was causing tears to well up in her eyes.

He chuckled bitterly. "Well, if you're blind, I am too. I can't see a damned thing either."

His statement offered a strange kind of comfort to her. The thought that she might be able to see after all brought a large wave of relief.

"We need to find a source of light," Mike went on, "so we can assess the situation better. Surely there will be help on its way, we just have to make do until they arrive."

Pain wracked her head and neck once more, but she felt comforted to know that he felt as she did. Again she was aware of the steady pelting of the icy rain on the outside of the plane, and sensed once again how cold she was.

"There must be a flashlight up front near the pilot's seat," Mike went on, "you'll have to try to find it."

She nodded in agreement, as if he could see her, and the pains felt more intense. "Ron?" she cried, trying to call the pilot.

"I've been trying to call him too," Mike said, "but so far, no luck."

Angela slid forward now, toward the source of the cold breeze, until she could touch the shoulder of the pilot. She shook him gently, as she had Mike, calling his name as she did.

No answer.

"Are you still awake, Mike?" she asked.

51

"Yes."

"He's not responding."

"I can tell," Mike responded patiently. "I wish I could help. There has to be a light there somewhere."

"I have an idea!" she offered. "He's a smoker. He has to have a lighter somewhere in his pockets!"

She then moved closer yet to the unresponsive pilot. Her hands began moving from one of his pockets to another. "I hope he's not offended by such familiarity," she said, trying to make light of the desperate situation. The pilot's body was covered by large amounts of sticky fluid, and Angela tried not to think about what that might be.

In his right jacket pocket she found it. "Here it is!" she cried.

Subconsciously she wiped her hands on the hem of her skirt, at the same time being careful not to drop the cigarette lighter she had found.

"How do you get this thing to go?" she asked, as she clicked the button up and down.

"Let me have it," Mike commanded, "it's probably child-proofed, and unless you have used one…"

Quickly she was back at Mike's side, and in no time he had a small blue flame going.

She could see his face in the glow. "I can see you," she reported. "I hope you can see me!"

He decided not to report on the ugly, lumpy gash he could see on her forehead. "I can see you too," he said quietly. He quickly showed her the secrets of operating the small source of light, then he said, "See if you can find a better source of light than this. I know Ron would have a flashlight where he could reach it."

"Gotcha!" she responded. A little enthusiasm showed in her voice.

He released the pressure on the little lighter, and it went out again.

Angela once again crawled toward the front of the plane, confident that she could start the lighter again once she was there. She was glad that she didn't have to touch the still silent pilot again.

Once in position she ignited the small light once more. She squinted as she scanned across the face of the dashboard. A glove compartment was to the right, but no flashlight could be found inside. She then looked between the front seats, and there was a small console there. She flicked open the door.

There it was! She could see that it was large enough to be a small spotlight.

Out went the lighter, and she picked up her find and turned it on.

The breeze from the front was a distraction, and she could feel the wet of the rain as it came in. It was very cold throughout the inside of the plane. Maybe there was something she could do to possibly close off the opening. She panned the cockpit area, swinging the flashlight back and forth.

Suddenly the beam of light focused on a sight more horrible than any she had ever seen before. She could not stifle the scream that built in her throat. She stared and screamed and screamed. Then she began to sob uncontrollably.

A tree branch had crashed through the left windshield, and pilot Ron Marks now had only half of a head, and no face at all!

Chapter 13

There was one man that Bo Vitilli trusted. Just one. Mac MacIlwaine.

They sat in silence as the incessant rain continued to rattle off the roof and windows. One small candle shed a tiny amount of light in the small living room. Shadows of three other men indicated their presence in the room also.

In an adjacent room that was also illuminated by candlelight, Farley, Pauly, and Vasily sat at a table. They had attempted to start a card game, but no one had been able to concentrate. The three men simply sat quietly.

"We have to assess this situation," Vitilli was saying. "We need a plan of action."

MacIlwaine drew on his pipe, as if the professorial killer was in deep thought. "I don't think we can stay here," he finally concluded. "Not for long anyway."

"I'm sure that the cops called in their position before they came up the drive way," he continued. "As soon as the roads are clear, there will be many visitors."

"That's the trouble," Vitilli said. "We can't leave either. Not with the roads as they are."

"The cops will have all kinds of communication," Mac was continuing. "they will know the weather conditions, the road conditions…"

"We can get a battery run radio, a scanner…"

"For what? So we can be ready for them armed with our paltry five pistols? We need to get out of here. Find a hiding place somewhere."

Vitilli had already assigned the policemen's pistols to Vasily and Martinson. The two men had killed before. They would know what to do.

Minutes before he had sent Martinson down the road he had come from, and it was already hopelessly blocked. The same could be said in the other direction. Pauly had taken a ride in his vehicle and had gone only a few hundred yards.

They were trapped, awaiting the road crews who would bring a batch of curious officers. It was obvious that the news of their drug ring was out. The cops would be here in full force, even with helicopters.

They had to disappear.

"Didn't you have combat training," Mac was saying, "some sort of survival stuff?"

Vitilli grunted a "yes" in response to the query.

"If we could go into the forest somehow, and emerge where Lyson has a hideout, we could get help," Mac went on, "Lyson is one of Cheese's boys, and Cheese will want to retrieve this shipment."

"You're right," Vitilli agreed.

Martinson was listening to the conversation in the darkness. "Why don't we just get some chain saws and cut our way through?"

Use your head," Woody retorted. "First of all, that would involve a tremendous amount of work, and don't forget the power lines!"

"And the cops are cutting through from the other side with much better equipment." Mac agreed, "We'll just meet them and have no place to run."

"When the weather clears up, we're dead meat," Woody replied, worriedly.

"We've got to get out of here, as soon as possible," MacIlwaine stated, once again.

Abdul was a silent one, and rarely offered to enter any conversation, but he as well as everyone else could feel the urgency of the situation.

He looked ominously at Vitilli, anger smoldering in his dark eyes. "You better come up with a plan!" he said.

Since the troopers had been killed, and they had re-entered the house, Vitilli had been spending a moment here and there studying an old map of the Adirondack Park. He laid it out again, and was silent for a moment or two.

Finally he slammed his palm on the map. "We can go on foot," he declared, and pointing to a spot on the paper, he went on, "we can work our way over here, where we have a few friends, and they can get us out of here."

"Walk?" Abdul sneered, "Through there? That's the cursed Couchsacrage!"

It was Vitilli's turn to be angry. "Well, you can stay here, then, and wait for the cops. It's up to you. I know a guy at Wolf Lake, near Bunchberry. He'll help us if we can get there."

"Supplies. We need supplies." It was Woody. Except for Vitilli, he was the most experienced outdoorsman.

"Just a mile down the road there is a fishing and hiking supply store. We can get what we need there." By the tone of his voice, everyone knew that the well-respected MacIlwaine was in favor of the decision.

"Then it's settled," Vitilli said. Then he shouted to the men in the adjacent room, "Pauly, Farley, Vasily. Get in here!"

Once all of his men were in the same room he ordered, "Everybody grab as much of the merchandise as you can and follow Farley. Put the stuff in those barrels buried in the ground out back of the barn. He'll show you the way."

"Cheese thinks of everything," stated Pauly. He, like most of the others, had never seen the gangster boss with the code name, but Pauly's sort admired this mystery criminal as some sort of godfather.

"And when you're done, hit the sack," Vitilli added. "We're up and out of here before daybreak."

Chapter 14

The chills that were running up and down Angela's spine seemed to be endless. And the pain in her head and neck continued to hammer away. It was hard to fight off the self-pity that engulfed her. "Why me?" she asked herself, typically.

Somewhere, in the dark, in front of her, laid the bloody remains of what, hours before, had been a laughing, friendly, competent man. Now half of his head was gone.

Nearby, to her right, slouched in a ball, laid her consort, Mike Howell, now apparently half paralyzed and unable to help her at all. He might even die.

The tears welled in her eyes. She hated where she was. She hated the darkness and the incessant freezing rain and the sound of the beat it made as it monotonously tinkled on the roof and sides of the demolished plane.

At this point she even hated being the governor's daughter. If he made a living in a different way she wouldn't be where she was right now.

Another cold breeze from the broken windshield made her shiver.

The tears were flowing freely now. She was so cold! All she had on was a skirt and a light blouse and light jacket. She was wearing fancy dress flat shoes, not suited to wallow about in the wilderness. She was thankful for her panty hose; at least her legs would be somewhat protected.

"Oh! What am I going to do," she wailed aloud.

"Miss Bartholemew?" Mike was awake.

"We're going to die!" she snapped. "Nobody will find us here! Let's face reality."

"What do you mean?" Mike asked, showing a little tremulousness.

"What can we do?" There was anger in her voice this time. "We're not exactly Lewis and Clark! We're stuck, in the middle of nowhere. We don't even know where we are! We could be in the middle of Quebec somewhere! Who'll ever find us? And look at the weather out there! Who'll even be able to look for us?"

To Mike she was whining, like a spoiled little rich kid. He responded to her acrimony with same. "Well, I'm not going to give up! I want to live! I'll drag myself out of here with my arms if I have to!" His words had a bite as they snapped her way.

His anger halted her bout with self-pity. Giving up made no sense at all, and she knew it. She sighed, and the tears stopped. His spirit had brought out the willingness to fight within her once more.

"All right!" She had a haughty tone this time. "What can we do? You are not going to crawl around and wait on me!"

"That's better!" Mike cheered her. He had his own fears; his own doubts: Crippled for life! Unable to walk ever again! Every time he tried to move his legs the panic seized him. He knew that he would have his own moments of despair. He would be leaning on her for emotional and spiritual support soon enough. He was sure of it.

For now, he would try to be strong for her.

Although it was totally dark, and the sleeting rain continued its maddening beat on the roof, they both realized that, at least for now, they had each other.

"I'm glad you're here," she said softly, "I couldn't face this alone."

"Same here," Mike answered. "With planning and luck and sheer grit we might get out of this mess. You know what they say…ten years from now…"

"We're never going to laugh at this!" Angela scolded, "because poor Ron is over there, his head…" she stopped with a sob that choked in her throat.

It was quiet then, for a moment.

"At least we aren't in the St. Lawrence River," Mike offered, "that would be a bummer."

"That's a comforting thought," she agreed, "and we could have caught on fire..."

"Look! See? Now we're counting our blessings!" he interrupted enthusiastically.

"Can they find us?" she wanted to know. It was time to face a little truth.

"These planes can radio exact longitude and latitude," Mike said. "I don't know if Ron had a chance to send those bearings or not. At any rate, there was a flight plan, and people will have an idea where we may be by dead reckoning along a line on a map."

Right then a large tree broke and fell right next to the plane, making a thunderous crash as it struck the ground. It was unable to carry the burden of ice that had formed on it.

"We'll probably be killed by a falling tree!" Angela cried.

"If our bearings are known," Mike continued, ignoring the events around him, "there may be help on the way right now."

"In this storm? How could they get here?"

"It may take a while, but they will be here."

"Nothing to worry about," she joked.

"Well," he chuckled, "I wouldn't go that far."

Once again she was aware of the cold breeze that came through the broken glass. A shiver ran down her spine, but she was aware that suddenly it was a physical discomfort rather than an emotional one. The conversation with Mike had made her feel better.

"It's cold in here," she said. "How can I get warm?"

63

"Well, we could cuddle," he joked. He also thought of how beautiful she was. Cuddling with her was an excellent idea.

"Don't be funny," she responded, feigning an indignant tone. "I hardly know you." But she allowed that there was wisdom in his suggestion.

"Seriously," Mike was saying, "there has to be an emergency kit somewhere on the plane. And Ron, at least, should have some spare clothes packed somewhere…"

"I could use some warm clothes." she sighed.

"Well, Ron's through with his!" Mike put in. He knew it sounded like a heartless statement, but the idea was a practical one.

She jumped. "I'm not going near that cockpit again for anything!" she exclaimed.

"I don't blame you," he said. "But you will need to find something warm to wear. You will have to do all of the physical work we need to survive!"

"Well, maybe when the sun comes up," she said with resignation. Then she turned and slid toward him.

"In the meantime," she said softly, "maybe we can cuddle a little."

Chapter 15

It was very early in the tiny village of Bunchberry. It was long before dawn would rise, or whatever excuse there would be for dawn in such grim, cold moist weather.

The Town Hall was located within what once was the Bunchberry High School. A small party of four had gathered inside, in preparation for the rescue mission that was about to embark.

Forest Ranger Pete Randolph was all business. He was tall, and straight, and wiry. He was a of a breed of outdoorsmen who could handle himself in any situation, who was a fervent skier, hiker, kayaker. He appreciated fully the wilderness, its challenges, its treasures.

To Dag Dagonneault, the man was maybe too high strung, too wrapped up in his own mission. There seemed to be no humor there, only passion.

It was Pete Randolph's fortune to be the only Ranger available in the Bunchberry area, and the New York State Department of

Conservation officers had placed him in complete charge of the rescue operation. He looked forward to the challenge with high energy and relish.

In all he felt that he was fortunate to have found a team to go with him that looked promising. State Trooper Rose Fernandez, although reared in the city, seemed cool and competent.

Doc Ginsberg, whose credentials seemed a little shaky, was a trained medical person who, Pete hoped, would hold up under stress, if he stayed sober. Besides, how bad could it be? All they had to do was patch up as well as they could whatever crash victims there were and wait until help could come.

Dagonneault was a loose cannon. Word around town was that he was a highly respected outdoor sportsman, particularly in areas of hunting and fishing. Pete had also been told that Dag knew the area in question as well as his own back yard, and that he could probably walk through this particular part of the Couchsacrage blindfolded.

Looking at maps was one thing. A man who could pick out important landmarks on the scene was invaluable.

But Ranger Randolph was aware that Dagonneault also harbored many bitter feelings toward what he called "outside interference in the rights of Adirondackers."

Pete anticipated a problem here. The trick would be to focus on the task on hand.

"My orders are to find the plane," he was saying, "and give aid to whoever needs it, until some sort of transportation can arrive."

"We have to walk?" Doc Ginsberg asked, "we can't use ATVs?"

"The land is classified!" Pete shot back in horror. "No motorized vehicles allowed! This is primitive wilderness!"

Dag grinned. "Even when the governor's daughter is at stake," he said mockingly.

Pete glared at him. The rift was already beginning. "Policy is policy," he sniffed, "and in that light the governor's daughter is no different than anybody else."

"Besides, it's bad politics," Dag put in, again not necessarily to please Pete at all.

"Look," Pete replied. "We have to concentrate on what we need to do here, not get sidetracked by things we have no control over."

Dag nodded in agreement. "Well," he added, "in regards to the ATV situation, you all should know that there is no possible road or trail left open and usable to this part of the Couchsacrage. As far as I know, the only way to get to that plane, is on foot."

It was Rose's turn to speak, "and Lord knows what the ice storm is doing to the path right now."

"There really is no kept path," Dag went on. "There used to be a road in there, on the top of an old railroad bed. I presume it is all grown up with vegetation, even trees. There were culverts there, to allow various brooks to cross under the road. They are probably washed out by now."

"Why would they wash out?" Rose asked.

"No maintenance," Dag answered, glaring at the forest ranger.

On a table in the back of the room were four packs, carefully prepared by the Forest Ranger.

"Let's check our gear," he beckoned, and he carefully reviewed each pack, carefully indicating rain gear, tents, sleeping bags, dried foodstuffs, cooking utensils, and all other necessities for the trip.

"Can you estimate how long it will take us to get there?" he asked Dag, in a friendly tone.

"It's hard to say exactly," Dag said, "a lot depends on what's blocking the way. I think we'll get to the plane sometime tomorrow."

"That's what I thought," Pete agreed. "By the way, there is room for personal stuff, especially extra clothes," he then said, referring to the packs again.

Then he reached for a box under the table. "The fire department is lending us these waders," he said. "They aren't too comfortable, but we can cross waist-deep water with these on."

"I'm not going to walk with those on," Doc protested.

Rose giggled. "We'll tie them to our packs and just use them when we have to," she smiled.

Once all the gear was in place, they all went about preparing for their long walk, dressing warmly with various layers of clothes, then the packs, snapping and tying all of the appropriate fasteners, then the ponchos.

Doc noticed that both Pete and Rose were wearing pistols. They would be just extra weight to him.

"Expect trouble?" he asked.

"Just part of our official uniform," Rose replied.

Moments later they were headed down the road, beams from their flashlights illuminating their path. They went past the boarded up hotel, past the little library, and when they got to the lonely Presbyterian Church, they turned left.

They were in single file, with Ranger Randolph in the lead. Before him was a small opening in the bushes, and an inconspicuous little path that disappeared into the sleet and the mist and the darkness.

Into the Couchsacrage.

Chapter 16

"Wow! That was close!" Angela cried.

Another tree had broken right next to the plane, the shattering of branches across the growing ice sheet causing a large amount of tintinnabulation.

"I can't sleep; I have to do something," she groaned. The throbbing in her head and neck had subsided some, but her stomach had commenced to growl, and her skeletal muscles were noticeably aching, possibly from the results of the crash. Due to her previous vexation she had obviously been ignoring other discomforts.

Besides, the plane seats were not exactly made for two people to huddle together.

She assumed her partner was still asleep. Still, she found herself leaning over him and whispering, "You were right, Mike, we will have to fight on."

She seemed to be having a big burst of energy, but as soon as she moved away from the warmth of Mike's body, she again felt the chill that ran through her from head to toe. The breezes from the broken windshield seemed to be mere zephyrs, but they were agonizingly cold.

She could hear the tinkling of precipitation across the roof. "This damned storm isn't going to let up, is it?" she muttered, mostly to herself.

Mike groaned and opened his eyes, to see nothing, of course. In a moment of hopefulness, he tried to move his legs once more. Nothing doing. Once again the great fear seized him.

But he thought of Angela, and determined that her mental state was shaky at best. It was better to present a positive demeanor. The best bet was to keep her occupied, busy at essential tasks of survival. "Thank God it's so dark," he thought, lest she detect the fear he felt would show on the features of his face.

"Hey! It's warmer with you over here!" he joked aloud, although he wasn't exactly kidding.

"Sorry, kid," she replied in the dark, "Let's formulate some sort of plan."

"Well, get your flashlight out," he suggested.

This brought a different kind of regret. When she had looked upon the poor deceased pilot, and began to scream hysterically, she had shut it off and put it down somewhere. But where?

"I don't know where it is," she said apologetically.

Mike let out a slow sigh. Keeping himself together and composed was not going to be easy.

71

"I know," she went on, "You doubt if I can be of any help at all. Maybe I have doubts of my own."

"Nonsense," he snapped, "C'mon Miss Bartholemew, you're the only hope I have."

Her voice brightened considerably. "You know," she replied, "We've already been cuddling together, you probably should call me Angela. Besides, I'm not royalty or anything, just a college kid."

Mike was thankful for the sudden easement of propriety. "Angela," he said, "Nice name. I always liked that name."

Angela giggled, "Well, my college room-mates don't call me Miss Bartholemew, that's for sure."

"What's your major?" he asked.

"Social sciences. I like to study people, different cultures, how to get along. How about you, Mike?"

"My main interest was playing hockey for Cortland. Along the way I majored in Social Studies. I thought I might like to be a teacher and a coach someday. But this job is okay."

"Up until now," she added. sadly.

He sighed again. "If you can't find the flashlight," he said, getting back to the present order of business, "perhaps you still have Ron's lighter?"

She slapped at the pockets of her jacket. "Yes, here it is! Now, to find the flashlight."

Almost immediately she found it, right behind the pilot's seat.

She flicked it on, and began to peruse the interior of the plane, avoiding as much as possible any views of the dead man in front.

"Certainly, somewhere...," she whispered, "Yes! A box!" She slid over to it immediately, and opened the latch and lifted the lid.

"Look Mike," she cried, "a lantern, and spare gas, a tarp, blankets, even spare food! Lots of stuff!"

"It sure beats Christmas," he replied.

Chapter 17

For many of Vitilli's men, it had not been easy to set all of their vehicles on fire.

Plates had been removed and buried in the barn, before that too had been set ablaze.

And then the old house went too.

"No evidence," Vitilli cried. "No fingerprints, no personal effects, nothing. If you can't carry it, burn it."

At the first sign of protest, Vitilli screamed, "Don't worry! Cheese will make it good."

The police car, with the dead officers piled inside, went up too. "Dead radios, dead men," Farley chuckled. "Let them start from scratch!"

"Well, not exactly scratch," worried Woody. On his back he carried his prized possession, an antique hunting rifle he had rescued from his truck. If anything was going to leave with him, it would be his pride and joy.

It would be daylight soon, and the eight drug runners trudged down the highway, illuminated at this point by the magnificent conflagration behind them.

As the misty rain continued to fall, and heavy ice relentlessly crystallized on limbs and branches throughout the wilderness, the men could hear many trees and parts of trees cracking and breaking all around them.

Two such trees had already fallen along the side of the road, crossing what had recently been their driveway, and creating a barrier that would hide the entrance to their former hide out for some time to come.

Meanwhile, a few miles down the road, Myron and Marie Arbur slept comfortably in the back room of their store. Arbur's Camping and Tackle Shop was their retirement haven.

Although the Couchsacrage was deep and somewhat impenetrable, there were plenty of opportunities for fishing and hiking and camping along the perimeter, and tourists often stopped by at the store for supplies before going about their business.

The store also had a good supply of automotive needs, because the area was so remote.

Myron and Marie took great pride in their little store. "If you need it, we got it," Myron often joked as travelers stopped to browse, or perhaps enjoy a soda and a microwaved hot dog.

Sometimes, particularly in winter, when the only customers were hardy snowshoers and cross-country skiers, things were mighty quiet around the little cabin. But the Arburs loved the woods, and they loved the solitude and the winter wildlife. Marie particularly loved feeding whatever little creatures came her way.

"Florida is for wimps," was another favorite saying of Myron's.

When business was really slow, Marie would often utter, "Thank God for those retirement checks!" But the couple did not need a lot of money to enjoy their lives.

Myron and Marie were very popular with everyone who knew them. They remembered names and faces well, as well as particulars about those who stopped by often. Myron also seemed to know all the best jokes that were going around, and was an excellent story-teller as well. Many salesmen and truckers made it a point to stop by, if only just to take a break before going on their way.

The ice storm did not worry this hardy couple. They had everything they needed to ride out the storm. "Don't worry, ma," Myron had announced just before crawling into bed, "I've got plenty of gas for the generator. What could go wrong?"

So the couple slept peacefully, without any fear whatsoever that any harm could come to them on that night.

It was Marie who heard the noise first.

They had anticipated the power going out, and had two bright battery operated lanterns by the bed. Marie turned one on and nudged her snoring husband.

"What?" he asked, annoyed.

"Breaking glass, up front," she said.

Myron sleepily swung his body to an upright position, and grabbed for his robe. Then he reached down and turned on his lantern. "Damned ice storm," he complained. Probably a tree branch or something."

"I hope the rain won't spoil some of our inventory," Marie worried, as she too arose from the bed, "hopefully we can get some tarps and cover things up."

Myron was already headed for the front of the store, mumbling something like "it was time to get up anyway."

"I'll make some coffee," she said.

"Try and get the generator going," he suggested.

A kitchen separated the bedroom and the store, and Myron hurriedly passed through, waving his lantern from window to window as he went.

It was upon entering the store itself where he was confronted by a dire problem. Many men were in there, scurrying about through the store's inventory. They had already placed numerous expensive backpacks near the door. On top he could see sleeping bags, tents, nesting pots, and other assorted gear.

Several men were trying on expensive sweaters, rain suits, and boots.

A smallish, dark complexioned man sat in front, near the cash register, reading aloud a list of things needed.

"What's going on here?" Myron cried.

Two men immediately drew pistols, an ugly dark man by the door and a tall gray haired man who was stationed by the fishing poles.

At that moment, Marie stumbled into the room, nearly running into her husband who had stopped so abruptly in his tracks.

"What is it?" she gasped. "You people, who are you? What are you doing?"

"Easy, lady," the tall man said, in a calm voice. "We need to borrow some things…"

"At gunpoint?" Myron shot back, disgustedly.

"Don't move," he was warned, again by the tall man.

The others had gathered a supply of everything Vitilli had read. He had tried to anticipate all of their needs. "To the clothes racks, men. Remember, it's cold and wet out there. And don't forget good boots."

"Hey!" Myron protested, "those jackets are worth hundreds of dollars!"

"Relax!" MacIlwaine warned.

As the men dressed hurriedly, Vitilli was once again on top of things. "Make sure you take all personal effects out of your old clothes. We don't want to leave any identification behind."

"Who are you people?" Marie asked, her voice aquiver with anguish and worry.

"We don't want to know," Myron warned steadily. "We don't need to know."

It was obvious to Myron that he and his wife were in great danger, but he could not think of any plan to alleviate the situation. He began to pray quietly to himself.

At this point, Abdul had put away his pistol and donned his stolen camping clothes. He had stopped at the main counter in the front of the store, fascinated by the brand new filleting knives on display there. He took the butt of his gun and broke the glass and helped himself to a nice one. He took it from its sheath, and tested its sharpness by running it carefully against the print of his thumb.

"Who's going to pay for this stuff?" Marie protested.

"Relax, lady," Vitilli snickered, "we got credit cards."

This brought a nervous chuckle from some of the other men.

"Remember," Vitilli advised, "We may be in the woods for three or four days. Bring enough food."

Myron could feel a cold sweat running down his spine. His survival instincts were taking over his mind, and he began to realize that he and Marie needed to get out of there, as fast as they could. He had no doubt that the thugs he could see before him would not want any witnesses.

Marie was trembling. She too could sense the danger, and was fearing for their lives. Visions of her children and her grandchildren flashed through her head.

By now, the men were packed, and each in turn grabbed what he had stolen and headed out the door.

Myron thought that the distraction would provide him and Marie a chance to escape, perhaps to hide in the forest until the danger had passed.

He took his wife by the hand, and they turned to head back through the kitchen.

Too late! A pistol exploded, held by the greasy, swarthy man who had been giving directions. Myron turned and fell, a bullet through his brain.

Marie screamed in anguish and shock and terror, and knelt down by her dead husband's side.

"Take care of her, Abdul," the swarthy man ordered.

The tall, dark, expressionless man reached in his coat for the filleting knife he had just taken from the display case in the front of the store.

In a moment Vitilli was back outside.

"Follow me," he ordered, and began to walk down the road.

The men followed.

But the silent ice storm could not drown out the agonized cries of the woman inside.

Then it was quiet.

Chapter 18

It was worse than he thought.

Dag Dagonneault quietly reprimanded himself. "What the hell did you expect? You should have had imagination enough to see how bad it was going to be in your mind's eye!"

The four rescuers were in single file. First there was Ranger Randolph, then Police Officer Fernandez, followed by Dag and Doc.

A dim gloomy light hung over the place. The clouds, just the least bit translucent, barely indicated a semblance of sun above their ragged cover.

The stinging of the frigid rain constantly provided a fine spray.

At their feet, at rare places where there weren't clinging branches and obstacles like roots and fallen trees, was a slick floor of ice and water, providing very treacherous footing. They had to move carefully.

In fact, "Move carefully," was the order of the day. "If you hurry to the point where you get injured," Pete Randolph had explained, "what possible use can you be when we arrive at the plane? We might not arrive at all, we'll have to rescue you instead."

A point well taken. The small group moved on in earnest, but also with a careful respect to the dangers of a twisted ankle, a poked eye, a broken appendage.

A good deal of the path was underwater, though not so deep that the firemen's boots were necessary, and through it all the little group from Bunchberry slogged on.

They were all wearing slouch hats, and waterproof gloves, and ponchos. For the most part, no matter how long they would need to stay out in this hostile environment, they would be able to stay warm and dry.

They wormed their way up, over and around bent and broken poplars, birches, and young trees of various species. Evergreens were now ice laden, and their limbs reached out from every direction to grab and cling with icy hugs. In some places, these branches tangled up with other branches from adjacent trees, making thick icy walls that blocked the narrow, hard to discern trail. Sometimes the party could crash through these obstacles, and sometimes they had to walk around, confronting other barriers as they went.

It was all very time consuming.

"What are we going to do when the trail peters out?" Dag asked, directing his question toward Ranger Randolph. As far as Dag could determine, Pete was the only other member of the party who would have some sort of knowledge of the topography that needed to be crossed.

"We have to head west," Pete answered. "We need to go to Chub Pond country."

Dag took offense to the answer. "No kidding," he replied, "if we weren't going to Chub Pond, I wouldn't be here."

They were at it again! Rose Fernandez shook her head. They certainly were different, Dag and Pete, she thought. Could they possibly have anything in common except for the love of the outdoors? Even in that context, they viewed the Couchsacrage so differently.

"There is almost no visibility," she observed out loud, "We can only see about fifty feet ahead."

"That's okay, Rose," Dag answered. "This isn't exactly the high peaks region here. It's all pretty much a flat swamp, and even in the sunlight you can't see very far. That's why so few sightseers come in here. Actually, nobody comes in here." There was a slight irony in his voice.

Pete Randolph caught the inflection. He stopped in his tracks, and turned to look at Dag. "That's just the point," he declared, "It's forever wild in here. It's classic northeast wetland. People shouldn't come in here."

"I sure wish that where you come from is wet land," Dag shot back, "Then they could close up your village and move your mom and pop off the land they grew up on and close it off so nobody would go there any more!"

"This land was bought because the voters wanted it that way. Democracy in action."

"That's a crock. It was all sneaky politics. The voters didn't want this at all. That's a fact!"

"Please!" Rose interrupted. "This conversation is not part of our main focus."

Pete Randolph glared.

"Sorry," Dag apologized, "You're absolutely right. I keep fighting a battle that's already been lost."

Then Dag turned to Pete. "Are you leading the way, or what? I know this much, at this rate we won't get to Chub Pond until tomorrow."

Pete nodded. Without further comment, he moved on, with the other three closely behind.

Into the dark mist, into the sleet, through the ice and mud and water, climbing over, up around and through broken stumps and branches.

Into the Couchsacrage.

Chapter 19

Miles away, on another path that led into the Couchsacrage, another group hastily meandered on, through the continuous drizzle, the mist, and the sleet and ice.

They also noticed the semblance of light that had begun to dimly illuminate the translucence above, and each member of this group, like those in the other, stepped cautiously around, over, and through bent over trees, bowed icy branches, and broken stumps.

In their case, however, there was an urgency to the way they went about their business, as if somewhere someone was pursuing them.

If the pace of the group from Bunchberry was tempered by caution, the possibility of injury was of little concern to anyone in Vitilli's party. To cross the Couchsacrage in the most expiditious way possible was their only goal. They didn't know of any plane crash. They didn't know of the rescue party far away in another corner of the swamp. They only knew that they needed to rescue themselves, from a law that would be breathing down their collective necks soon enough. With a sense of urgency, they pushed on.

As soon as the weather cleared, police would be everywhere to hunt down the killers of two young police officers and the elderly Arburs.

They would be combing through the burnt buildings and vehicles, looking for clues. There would be nothing that would escape their attention.

There were thousands of dollars worth of hidden drugs in the woods near their former hide out, and Vitilli was sure that Cheese would be greatly unhappy if all was lost.

Soon cops might even surround the Couchsacrage, with armed officers at every trail-head, and Vitilli knew that a swift passage was in their best interest. Wolf Lake was near Bunchberry, and he had to find the quickest way to get there. One of Cheese's most trusted lieutenants lived nearby, and could help them.

Time was the enemy.

But as Vitilli moved on, he also realized that the ice storm was his friend. As long as it continued, and as long as power was out and the road was closed, he had time. As far as he was concerned, the ice storm could continue on for several days more.

Still, he wanted to be free of the Couchsacrage as soon as was possible.

At this point the trail had been fairly easy to travel, and as each man made his way into the Couchsacrage, he could reflect on the deaths they had witnessed during the past twenty-four hours.

For some it was simply perfunctory, like brushing one's teeth, "all in a day's work," so to speak. They had taken part in executions before, and to these men what had happened was no big deal at all.

Bo Vitilli was such a man. The policemen and the elderly couple had merely been obstacles who undoubtedly would have fingered the members of the gang in a court of law. Even though the killings had taken place just hours before, he had already relegated the memories in his mind to a place he conceived as proper perspective. There was no point in delving on a necessary act of violence.

Woody was next in line, and he looked at the entire chain of events in a totally different way. He could still see the fear in the eyes of Marie and Myron Arbur, proud people who had worked hard for a living all of their lives. Thoughts of his own grandparents flashed through his mind, and he regretted his role in the entire affair.

Next came Farley, a nervous slight little man with long hair and a grubby stubble of a beard. Gunfire and blood were a kind of elixir to him. Watching others in fear and in pain was a fascination for him, and he never gave it one moment of thought what it would be like to be on the receiving end. The events of the day had been quite thrilling.

Quiet, dignified MacIlwaine was next. At one time he had been a summa cum laude student in a prestigious university, a potential doctoral candidate. Strange and complicated turns had influenced his life, and now he was a professional killer. So warped was he that he thought only of the job, and doing it better than anyone else. The recent murders were all part of the job he was hired to do. That's all.

Smirky, bland Martinson was next in line. He had a face that was continuously contorted in a weird smile, like he was thinking of something that he should share, but he wasn't going to. In this world of drug dealing and cold-blooded murder, he was a willing novice. He was working his way up the ladder. Someday he planned to be a trusted assassin like MacIlwaine, the man he most admired.

To Abdul, the killings meant nothing at all. In his country, it was common to deal with one's enemies in this way, even if their indiscretions had been of a minor nature. He hated all Americans, and secretly wished they were all dead. He had many comrades who felt as he in distant Afghanistan, and he was in America to raise money to help their cause. He hoped he could help to overthrow and defeat the "great Satan of the west."

Pauly was next, his bewhiskered chin white with the drug he had just indulged in. Pauly was an inferno of changing emotions, and sober he might feel a certain remorse for what had happened. But sober was a rare condition for him, and he needed money and position to feed his addictions. The deaths, in this context, had been necessary.

The last man in the line was Boris Vasily. Where he came from it was not uncommon for one ethnic group to suddenly rise against another, with widespread murder, even of innocent women and children, a common practice. His whole being had been calloused into not caring, and nothing that had happened recently had changed anything.

Most of the men in the line were careful about addictions. In this group of men profit was the main motive. There were no hard core addicts in the group, although many carried portions of marijuana or crack, in case some was desired. In all, it was a pretty clean bunch, except, of course for Pauly, who already had too much of a need for substances that could consume his soul.

The eight fugitives moved forward, down into the swamp as fast as the terrain would allow. The Couchsacrage was not a casual walk even in the best of times, and this was the worst. Ice, darkness, slipperiness, and cold, were everywhere, from the footing underneath to the trees and branches that impeded their progress.

They were getting close to Hawk's Nest Pond. At that point, the trail would peter out, and after that they would be on their own, at the mercy of Vitilli's navigating skills.

Vitilli'd had survival training in the U.S. Army, and he was confident that, with his compass and his trusty old map, he could lead his men across the Couchsacrage. Sloshing through the ice-cold water, he moved ahead.

The events of the day bothered Woody a great deal. "Damn!" he finally exclaimed, mostly to himself, "Did you have to kill those old people?"

Vitilli had never been able to read Woody well. Woody was a great driver, and a highly efficient deliveryman. There was no doubt that he was an important asset to the organization. But still, to Vitilli, Woody was a weak link.

Immediately, Vitilli was on the defensive. "They saw us. They could connect us with the dead cops. They were very dangerous and could put us all away. They had to go."

"Did you have to turn Abdul loose on that poor woman? Didn't she at least deserve to die an easier and a more dignified death?"

"Shut the hell up," was Vitilli's enraged response. "If I hear any more about it I'll turn Abdul loose on you!"

The group continued on. Since Vitilli and Woody were in the lead, nobody else had heard the conversation.

In time, as the sleety rain continued, they arrived at the shore of Hawk's Nest Pond, and they worked their way around to the right. There were no trails beyond this point. Vitilli reached for his compass. "Now it will be really challenging," he thought.

They would try to make a beeline along a set course through the dense and swampy Couchsacrage, a feat that would be impossible even during the best of times. Vitilli was already embarking on what could not be done.

He turned to Woody and hissed, as the freezing rain dripped from his hat. "We'll wait here for the others. It will be rough going from now on, and we'll need to stick close together."

Chapter 20

Since the crack of dawn, Angela had been a busy girl.

Step one: she had to make Mike as comfortable as possible. She already had wrapped two of the newly discovered blankets around him.

"Do you need anything else?" she asked.

"I'm fine," he replied. "You only have to keep me warm from the waist up."

She could sense the bitterness he felt.

"Don't forget," he continued, "I can't feel a damned thing in my legs."

"All the more reason to keep them warm," she lectured, "We won't be having frozen extremities."

"Now you sound like a nurse."

"I've had first-aid training. I'm not a complete ignoramus in that department."

Step two: she had to find some warm clothing for herself.

This turned out to be easier than she thought. In her search through the plane she found a duffel bag, something that Pilot Marks had packed for himself for such an emergency.

And there was a cell phone! Eagerly she tried it. But nothing was going through. She hurriedly brought it to Mike.

He tried. There was no signal, nothing at all. It was dead. He had no technical knowledge of the workings of the thing either, so at the present at least, it was of no use to them.

They both cursed their bad luck. The plane radio system had been destroyed by the crash, and now they had found a phone that did not work.

"Oh well," Mike sighed. "If we can keep warm and comfy until help arrives, I guess it won't make any difference."

"Yeah," she agreed, and added realistically, "No help can come until the storm clears anyway."

She fished in the bag some more, and came up with a set of spare clothes and some boots.

Quickly she pulled a sweatshirt over her blouse. Then she donned a plaid flannel shirt and buttoned it. The change was apparent. Already she felt warmer.

"Close your eyes," she ordered Mike, and with that she pulled off her skirt, and replaced it with a pair of water- proof sweat pants she had found, pulling them up over her panty hose.

"Thank God there's a draw string!" she said, noting how baggy she was going to look. She tied the string tightly about her waist.

"Boots! These darned boots are too big!" she complained. "An extra pair of socks might help."

There were plenty of socks. With no small effort due to the confined quarters, she carefully removed Mike's dress shoes and put heavy socks on his feet.

"That ought to help your circulation," she said.

"You're so kind," Mike commented, "And I must confess, I peeked when you took off your skirt."

She feigned annoyance, "Who cares! I guess that proves that you are still an all-American lecherous boy!"

Strapped to the wall near the other supplies she found a small chain saw, a can of gasoline, and some bar oil. She brought the saw to Mike.

"We will probably have to set up some sort of heating system," she said. "Show me how to run this thing and I'll get some fire wood."

Mike's lecture was quite thorough, dealing not only with the operation of the device, but with safety as well.

"Are you sure you feel competent to run it?" he finally asked.

"If I don't, who will?" she replied.

He sensed that the machine frightened her. But he admired her for the fact that she recognized what needed to be done, and what her responsibilities might be. Angela Bartholemew was not the sort to sit around for long and feel sorry for herself.

Soon she was outside in the rain, and to Mike's surprise he could hear the whirring saw just outside of the wind shield in front of the wrecked aircraft.

Suddenly the plane lurched sideward, and listed badly. Then Mike heard a snapping sound, and the plane twisted and dropped several feet. Once again it came to rest, but this time on a side hill. His position was now precarious, his body hanging awkwardly to the left, only his seat belt holding him in place.

Terror gripped him. Whatever his injury, surely it is far worse now!

"Oh no! Oh no!" he could hear Angela crying, "What have I done!"

Chapter 21

Rose Fernandez wasn't exactly in charge of the rescue party. By law, Forest Ranger Pete Randolph led the operation. But as a police officer she felt that she certainly was allowed some authority, as well as an advisory power. She was concerned about the rift growing between the forest ranger and Dag Dagonneault. They were both expert woodsmen and they knew the Couchsacrage and its idiosyncrasies. If they could only work together.

Walking through the downed trees, the ankle deep water and ice, the grasping, clutching balsams and spruces, was all very taxing. When he found a spot of high ground, Pete called for a rest.

Rose noticed that Dag had struck up a conversation with Doc Ginsberg, and they were resting on a broken off top out of earshot from where she and Pete sat on an ancient log. She decided to take advantage of the situation.

"Pete," she began, "Can we talk?"

The ranger turned to her. He could see that, in spite of the garb she wore, here was an earnest and beautiful woman, and one he respected a great deal.

"Yes, Rose?"

"You can't fight with Dag. We need both of you and what each can offer this operation."

"That guy annoys the hell out of me!" Pete replied. "He doesn't even try to see the true picture of the conservation movement. He only talks of times past."

"His family settled here long ago. He's lost a lot. He feels that outsiders took his rights as surely as the rights of Native Americans were taken years ago."

"Well, times change. You can't get in the way of progress."

Rose's voice was a bit sterner now. "Well, I'm not going to pull any punches if this rescue is screwed up because of some personality conflict. You can argue about your philosophy if you want, but you'd better use what he knows and what he has to offer."

It was Pete's turn to get huffy. "Tell the same thing to him. I'll go along with it."

So she then got up and moved to where Dag was sitting, discussing the quirks of Adirondack meteorology with the medic.

"Can I talk to you, Dag?" she said firmly, but politely. She knew she outranked him, but pulling rank on the likes of a Dag Dagonneault would not necessarily be productive. Sugar instead of salt was the best approach here.

"You need to get along with Pete," she said. "We all need to work as a team."

"Well, he should have more respect for the people who settled the Adirondacks, and the sacrifices they made to make a place for their descendants here."

"He's impossible, I know," Rose agreed, "but we can't lose sight of the downed plane, and the fact that there may be survivors who need us."

"If he'll stick to the terrain, and how to cross it, so will I," Dag promised.

"That's fine," Rose smiled, her dark eyes flashing. "I appreciate that, Dag."

When she stood up to leave, she could hear him ask, "I don't really have to like that son of a bitch do I?"

She had no answer. With a shrug she walked away.

Chapter 22

The discernable trail ended at Hawk's Nest Pond. In better weather, family groups and Boy Scouts and Girl Scouts and other assemblages of people walked in to enjoy its scenic shores and picnic or camp. On a nice day, one would notice that it was just a small, scenic, clear Adirondack pond.

Today it could just as well be an ocean, for all one could see while looking out across its choppy waters was an ominous cloudbank just a few yards away.

"This is the end of the marked trail," Vitilli announced in a loud commanding voice, so everyone could hear. "It will be more dangerous now. We're going to move forward in single file. Don't lose sight of the guy in front of you. This wet sloshy crap leaves tracks for a while, but as the weather keeps coming down, they will disappear. Once you fall behind, you might never find us again.

"If you can't see the guy ahead, let out a shout, and we'll pass it down the line until we all stop, and you can catch up. And everybody should look back often, and also shout if you can't see the guy behind you. We can stop the line anytime and make sure all are accounted for."

Woody could almost see something admirable in Vitilli's paternal concern. But to Vitilli, each man was a valuable employee, hard to replace, nothing more.

Vitilli had one last warning. "Leave the drugs alone." He glared at Pauly. "This is no place to go on a toot."

Vitilli reached for his compass once again, and the ratty old map he carried. Woody wondered why Vitilli hadn't grabbed a new up to date map at Arbur's store.

Once again, Vitilli turned to the men. "With the visibility we have, I won't be able to focus on any long range land mark, so I'll be stopping often."

Then he moved forward, and the eight thugs slid further into the Couchsacrage.

The first part of the journey was across a hardwood stand, a slightly higher ground above the flatness of the wetland below. Across this area, the visibility was good enough so that they could keep moving. Keeping track of the man ahead was easy. This area had tall trees, big maples and beech and oak, not easily bent over. Still, the ground was strewn with branches and trees that had fallen, recently and in the past, and each man had to watch his footing.

The sleet continued to make the footing slippery, and they sloshed through quietly, but in some haste. Each man, with his head down, watched for obstacles while icy water dripped from his hat. They were in this order now: Vitilli, MacIlwaine, Farley, Martinson, Woody, Abdul, Pauly, and then Vasily.

Vitilli's eyes flashed eagerly. Orientation was something he had enjoyed as a serviceman. He had a passion for it, and there was no doubt in his mind that he could lead his men safely and quickly across the Couchsacrage.

"This should be easy," he said to his pal, MacIlwaine.

"I hope you are right," the Scotsman answered. Mac could feel a chill down his back, and he was sure that it wasn't caused by the storm.

Farley was taking it all a lot less seriously. He called back to Martinson, "When we get out of here and get paid, let's go to Montreal. I know a great whorehouse there, and they really treat you good!"

"You know where they are all right," Martinson agreed. "You even found a good one in Buffalo. It was really high class. Good booze, good drugs, good sex. Yep, the place had it all."

Woody was silent. He adjusted the strap that held his old hunting rifle across his back. There was no way that he would have left this prize behind. Again he wished that he had never been involved in all of this. Maybe someday he could get away, maybe get a cabin in Ontario, maybe get a good honest job, marry a nice girl, go hunting and fishing when he wanted to.

He was concerned at how well armed the others were. It was Vitilli and MacIlwaine who had killed the cops, and Vitilli had shot the old man in the store. These men were cold-hearted killers, and would shoot anybody they thought of as a threat.

Abdul, who was trudging right behind him, was a complete psychopath. Just having him near gave Woody the chills. The mysterious Abdul was very dangerous, that was for sure.

The two ambushed policemen had each had pistols, the regular issue. Boris Vasily and Hank Martinson had been given custody of these firearms. Woody presumed that Vitilli figured that, among the drivers, those two men would most likely be counted on if the trek across the Couchsacrage resulted in a gun fight with policemen at the other end.

He, Hal Woody, had no desire to shoot it out with the police. He would, if that happened, retreat back into the swamp. It would make him a marked man in Vitilli's eyes, this he knew. But he wasn't going to shoot any cops, that's all there was to it.

As he walked along in the mist and the ice, Woody wished he could be somewhere else, anywhere else.

Chapter 23

Angela was horrified. Panic surged through every inch of her body. She had been able to get the side door below the dangling Mike open, and she looked up from the hatchway. She sobbed uncontrollably.

"Oh Mike," she cried, "Are you okay?"

"What the hell were you doing?" Mike answered angrily.

So far he had been able to put up a brave front regarding the potential injury he had suffered. But the recent jarring had tried his patience. Now genuine fear had returned. Adrenaline was again rushing through his system. He had been resolved to ride things out until help came, and he knew very well that moving about and bouncing around was the last thing he should be doing. Now he was dangling from his seat belt in a wrecked plane that now seemed to be lying in its side.

"If I have hurt you worse I will never forgive myself," she sobbed. Pure anxiety was apparent on her every feature. Even her body language reflected her concern.

"Well, you've done the damage," Mike snapped, unforgivingly, "and I can't just hang like this. You'll have to unhook me. Goddam! If I wasn't paralyzed before, I sure as hell am now!"

He had been angry before in his lifetime, but this brought things up to a whole new level.

Angela felt helpless. Even if she loosened his belt, he would fall toward her, possibly banging against something else before he stopped. Things could get even worse.

"Get a rope!" he yelled, "In the emergency supplies case. A rope! Quit standing there frozen in space!"

She did as he had told her. When the plane had fallen, the case had popped open. She had to climb through some debris to get to it.

She passed the rope up to him, and he busily tied one end to the seat arm above him.

As he looked down, Mike could see nowhere to put himself. Everything that had been loose when the plane moved was scattered randomly about underneath him. There wasn't a level place to lay down, or to sit.

"I'm going to have to be out doors," he declared, "in this damned weather. I'll need the air mattress laid out for protection, and spread a tarp out on the ground."

The mattress was one of the self inflating kind, and in no time she placed it where she thought it was most likely he might bang against something.

"Wait!" she cried. She had discovered a second air mattress. This she inflated as well, and placed it along the casing that went around the hatchway.

"Good," he commented. "My arms are strong enough to lower myself to those mattresses, but you will have to guide my legs so that I don't make any unnecessary movements."

She took a deep breath. "Okay!" she said bravely.

It was a lot of responsibility, and she knew that she had brought a lot of this on herself. She prayed that he was not hurt worse because of her actions.

She climbed up to where she could grab his ankles.

"You ready?" he asked.

While holding the rope in his right hand, he popped open the seat belt fastener with his left. Quickly, he grabbed the rope with his left as well, then, hand under hand, and with Angela guiding his legs, he lowered himself toward the mattresses.

At one point they had to pause while she climbed down through the hatchway so they could continue. This was an agonizing moment for Mike, as his arms were tired, and he had to hold still, suspended as he was, until she got into place.

Finally he was on the tarp on the ground under the plane. Hurriedly she positioned bags and blankets to prop him up as comfortably as she could.

Still, he didn't like the plane precariously perched above his head. He wondered if a gust of wind might dislodge it and send it crashing down. What if more ice would break branches that were currently holding the plane in place?

"The way my luck is going," he mused sardonically, "it's just a matter of time before I'm hit in the head by an airplane."

Angela was lying beside him now, tears flowing down her cheeks.

"I'm so sorry," she grieved, "so sorry."

"What the hell were you thinking of!" he snapped.

But he really didn't want to scold her any longer. He was already setting aside his self-pity. He began to feel compassion for her, for he could sense the genuine concern and remorse that she felt.

To be fair, he had to cut her some slack. She had been trying to be helpful, and things had gone unpredictably wrong. The whole event was really the result of her lack of experience, and nothing more.

He reached for her and pulled her to him. She placed her face against his jacket and cried and cried.

"It's all right," he said, "it's all right."

Chapter 24

The forest floor was now dipping downward, and Ranger Pete Randolph was sure that soon they would be entering a great marsh that hunters once called Neverending Swamp.

This wetland went on for miles and miles, and even in the sunniest of days there were no landmarks to be used for bearings. All navigation would be done by frequent compass readings and by dead reckoning.

With this in mind, he stopped to take a compass reading. The hardwood plateau they had been crossing had dwindled down to a mere peninsula. He wanted to make sure that they would enter the swamp at the best place.

"What do you think?" he asked Dag, who came up behind him. At Rose's request, they were holding to a tenuous truce.

"Cobble Creek will be off to our left somewhere," Dag pointed, as the icy rainwater ran down his face. "When we reach it, go downstream. We should come to a place where a culvert runs under an old railroad bed. It might still be there. We can walk the bed right across to Chub Pond country."

Pete nodded. It was as he had expected. He moved on, with the others close behind.

As they began to cross the swamp they were considerably hindered by the low hanging, icy alders and spruces. There was either an impediment to step over or around, or the cold clinging needles of branches that had frozen together, creating barriers to be dealt with. The footing was also tricky, as their boots could not get a very good grip on the slushy ice. The misty cold, sleeting rain continued to fall.

Dag's mind slipped back in time, to when a road had been developed above the railroad bed. He remembered that hunters and fishermen of all ages had crossed through here, regardless of missing limbs or bad hearts. The land had been open for all to enjoy.

In winter, happy snowmobilers had once crossed through here, entire families enjoying recreation time, going from one restaurant to another, making a day of it.

He could almost hear the ghostly whir of their motors, and the joyous laughter of the participants.

They were all gone now. Gone forever.

When they got to Cobble Creek they found it to be overflowing its banks. Cautiously they gave the rushing water a wide birth, and their meandering compounded their navigating problems. Swamp brooks always have an infinite number of tributaries and backwaters lacing through the marsh along their banks, and the rescue party had to weave around these obstacles, lest they be forced to walk through icy chest deep water or worse. In all it forced the party to make what seemed to be endless zigzags that lead nowhere. And everywhere were the clutching branches and tripping alders.

It took awhile to get to where the culvert had once been. As Dag had feared, it had washed away, long ago.

Through the mist they could see the high ground where the gravel and the railroad ties held the old road together, but they could also see a gap through which hundreds of gallons of icy water rushed through every second.

Dag estimated that the hole was at least thirty feet across.

"What would make it wash out like that?" Rose asked.

"Probably beavers," Dag answered. "They block up the culvert, and water rushes over the road instead of under it. Floodwaters will tear out a culvert, and a big hole is formed."

Doc Ginsberg was a quiet man, not prone to long conversations, but he scratched his head in wonderment. "I don't think we can get across," he said. "Even if it was warmer, I don't think we could swim in that current."

Pete Randolph rubbed his chin in thought. The rescue mission was done, right then and there, unless they could get across the brook.

"Maybe it gets narrower upstream," Rose offered.

"Who knows how far we would need to go, in all of this mess?" Pete answered. "It might take a very long time to find a crossing."

Then Pete turned to all three of his fellow travelers. "Keep track of the brook so you don't get lost," he said. "We need to find a fallen tree, a softwood, perhaps a spruce. It has to be long enough to bridge that gap."

Windstorms are common in the Couchsacrage, and trees fall all of the time. The floor of Neverending Swamp continuously gets a supply of downed tree trunks, strewn about the place like a giant's game of pick up sticks. Anyone who had crossed the swamp in times past had had to deal with these endless impediments.

A tree that has been down for some time, especially a spruce, will lose considerable weight, and Pete hoped that the small party just might be able to move such a log about.

Rose Fernandez had only traveled a hundred feet and she found what they were looking for. It was long, seemingly sturdy, with plenty of ice covered branches.

The party was equipped with two very sharp bow saws, and they each took turns as they stripped the branches from the tree. It was obvious that the thing would easily bridge the gap in the railroad bed.

"Don't cut the branches all of the way back to the trunk," Pete ordered. "We will need the stubble for footing and for balance, especially with the ice forming on it."

The log was not all that heavy. With some grunting and huffing and puffing, and tripping and sliding, they managed to move it to the bank of the stream.

Now, to get it across.

"Any ideas?" Dag asked, looking around. "We can tie this end tight, and float the other end upstream until it hits the other bank…"

"You'll have water splashing across it," Doc was saying. "It would be very hard to cross."

Meanwhile Pete had the rope in his hand, and he was lashing one end to a forked stick. Then he commenced to heave the stick across the brook to the other side. He had a clump of short thick spruces as his target, and each time his stick would bounce off of them he would retrieve it and throw it again. Finally, it caught on something, and he pulled and pulled until he was satisfied that it would hold fast.

He handed the rope to Doc, "Keep the tension!" he ordered.

Then he began to take off his clothing. In no time he was standing naked in the cold, freezing rain. If Rose's presence bothered him it did not show.

In a flap on the side of his pack he found a plastic bag. In it he stuffed his boots and socks and as much clothing as he could.

"I'll need some kind of a towel," he muttered.

"Allow me," Doc replied, and produced a spare flannel shirt from the top of his pack. This Pete placed in the bag with his own clothing.

Then he took the other end of the rope from the coil that was on the ground, and tied the bag to it.

"When I reach the other side," he said to Doc, "set the bag carefully in the water. I'll want to put these clothes back on right away."

"I'm sure you will," Doc agreed.

Once again Pete took the rope in his hands.

"Everybody hang on to this end as tight as you can!" he ordered. Then he entered the water.

All three of his traveling companions shuddered at the thought of how cold the water must have felt.

Pete's biggest problem was fighting the current. He fell twice, but held fast to the rope, and scrambled to his feet again. A gravelly bottom does offer a certain amount of good footing.

Then he stepped in a hole, and disappeared momentarily, but again his head broke the surface, and hand over hand he fought his way to the distant shore.

Instantly the bag of clothes was set adrift, and Pete swiftly pulled it to him. "He looks absolutely blue!" Doc marveled.

There was a pause while Pete dressed himself. The ranger did not waste a moment nor make a false move while he rapidly completed his task.

Once his boots were tied once again, Pete grabbed the rope and threw one end back across the creek. Dag tied it to the forward end of the tree.

Then, with Pete pulling, and the others lifting and pushing, the log, with one end in the swift current bobbing up and down, soon traversed the gap.

The back end was nearly atop the railroad bed, high and dry. The other end, where Pete was, was still in the water. It presently was stuck to the bank, but its position was temporary at best.

Pete sat on this end, his legs holding the log in place. He waved to them to come on over.

Rose and Doc grabbed their packs, and one at a time, carefully crossed the teetering narrow log-bridge. They were thankful for the extra footing provided by the branch stubble. Already ice was forming on the bark.

Dag came over last, and in addition to his own pack, he carried Pete's as well.

"My hat is off to you; you did a helluva job!" he said to the ranger when he handed him his pack.

"The next one is yours," Pete winked. Already he was soaked again from the waist down, because he had straddled the log during the crossing. He only had one more dry change of clothes left in his pack.

There was reason to worry. Dag could think of at least two more culverts between where they were and Chub Pond.

"One last thing," Pete said. "Let's get this end of the log up on high ground. We might need it again."

As they lifted the end of the log toward the top of the bank, Dag could only wonder, "Why would we ever come back this way?"

Chapter 25

Trying to cross the Couchsacrage, without any previous knowledge of the land, was a fool's mission.

Vitilli was, in this case, the fool. By now he had crossed the hardwoods, and dropped down into the marsh. He and his party were a long way from where the rescuers were, and they were in a different swamp, but all the other characteristics were the same. Blow down, holes, stumps and roots, backwaters, rivulets and mud flats, and the ever present frozen sagging grasping branches forced the party to constantly make adjustments to their line of march.

Vitilli knew exactly what direction he wanted to go, but something was always in the way. No sooner had he and his group meandered around one obstacle, and he set the true course once more, another impediment presented itself. It went on and on.

There were many small brooks to cross, a little too wide and a little too deep to comfortably wade, so a shallower spot, or a place where there was a log or a beaver dam had to be found. Sometimes narrow places, which could be jumped, were before them. But as far as Vitilli and the others were concerned, this did not happen often enough.

Time, it all took time. The day was moving along, and nobody in Vitilli's party was impressed with the progress. Most of these men were not outdoorsmen. They were used to modern conveniences and comforts, and they were not happy at all. A sort of controlled panic set in, and the pace quickened.

The seven men who had willingly followed Vitilli into the mist, were by now at his mercy. He held the compass, and without a compass, not even Woody could have worked his way out of the morass.

But even the compass itself was getting under Vitilli's skin. It seemed as though every time he looked at it, the needle evilly pointed in a different direction, as if the instrument itself had taken a sinister persona, and was intent to lead them all to their doom.

He told himself that it simply meant that, because of the obstacles, they kept circling around. Still, he hated to think about it. He secretly hoped for some high ground. Maybe then he could set a straight course.

They entered a thick icy spruce grove, where the frozen branches held tight, making little closet sized openings. Through here every man had to be especially careful to keep track of the man ahead of him. There was a lot of shouting as the men fought their way through.

"Jesus! Don't you have any goddammed idea where you are going?" the frustrated MacIlwaine yelled. Ice dripped from his cheek. He had just been slapped in the face by a low hanging fir branch.

"Shut the hell up," Vitilli snarled back, his temper flaring. "If you think you can do better, you can take the lead. Or, better yet, you can go off on your own. I'm sick of you anyway."

Vitilli had always had a quick temper, and this situation was testing it completely.

Every man was worried as they followed Vitilli on his serpentine path, and every man would gladly have struck out on his own if he dared, in order to escape this cold hell of a place. Still, the only hope was to follow Vitilli.

"I must have died and gone to purgatory," thought Woody. He wondered if he would ever be able to atone for his sins. In addition he wished he could remove his pack and rest. The rifle case, worn under the pack, was causing an uncomfortable pull on his shoulders. He could feel a rash developing on his skin, due to the irritation.

Woody's thoughts went back to the murdered storekeepers. Remorse set in again. He rationalized that he had only taken what he thought he needed to survive. Now he wished he had taken one thing more, a compass of his own.

The panicky group kept moving. In the rain and in the sleet, Vitilli constantly changed direction.

Martinson, Farley, and the rest followed grimly, almost blindly. By now, even with the stolen boots, their feet were sore and cold. It was hard to think positively. Each wanted out but nobody dared to go it alone.

The weather showed no signs of changing, and the dark depressing mist encircled them everywhere. They could hear trees cracking, breaking, falling in the distance. This added to the terror of it all.

Abdul remained stoic, glaring ahead, features unchanged. Of all the men, he was the only one who had not yet complained.

The others looked at him apprehensively. He was a man to fear.

Life had never been easy for Abdul. He had no zest for life, and never seemed to enjoy anything. He plodded on.

"If you lose sight of the man ahead of you, give a shout," Vitilli had warned them. "We don't want to lose anybody."

Pauly Overton was deeply depressed, and when that happened he habitually smoked a joint or took a whiff of coke. The latter was his drug of choice at the moment, so he reached into his jacket pocket and produced what he needed.

It only took a moment to do what he had to do, but when he looked up, Abdul seemed to be way ahead. Pauly quickened his step to catch up. He felt a certain burst of energy.

The man at the end of the line was Boris Vasily. His mind had wandered back to the days of his Russian ancestors. "They lived in dampness and in extreme cold," he thought. He hoped he could reach back to them to help him now.

Sometimes accumulated ice, especially that attached atop a conifer, breaks loose and falls as if it is one unit. Poor Vasily. As he lurched ahead, a frozen sheet fell upon him, and the shock of this mass stunned him briefly. To make matters worse, he tripped over a root, and went sprawling atop the slippery ground.

To stand back up while wearing a full pack was a struggle.

By the time he was back on his feet and reoriented, he realized that Pauly was out of his sight. He called out, and frantically searched for foot prints on the ground.

The ice that had fallen from the tree had obliterated any tracks for several feet. He circled about, calling for help as he went about it.

Finally! A footprint! Thank God! Nervously he moved forward, trying to rapidly follow the marks that were already filling in due to the precipitation that continued to fall.

"Help! Help! Hey, wait for me! Hey! Hey!"

In the mist each footprint was almost individually stamped. Sometimes it took a moment to find the next one. He feared that the line ahead was moving at a greater pace than he was. He tried to go faster, but he did not dare to venture too far from the last track he had found.

Up ahead, Pauly was concentrating on Abdul. He knew that Abdul would not come back for him if he were lost. He wasn't even sure if Abdul would call for help if he needed it. Abdul was presently walking faster, and he had to keep up.

Pauly thought that he heard Vasily's voice, and he looked back to find him. Then there was a crashing caused by ice falling from branches. A chill ran down his spine. Survival! He had to keep up with Abdul, and Vasily had to keep up with him. Above all, he couldn't lose track of Abdul. He moved on.

The misty rain made a pitter-patter on the thick vegetation.

By now, Vasily was rushing too fast. To quicken his pace, he threw off his pack in order to make himself lighter. Once he rejoined the group, he thought, he would have to share whatever the others had. Catching up was of the highest priority. He even thought of discarding the policeman's pistol that he wore, but this he rejected. He was quite sure that he would need to use it later.

The tracks ahead were getting harder and harder to follow, and to make matters worse, the ground ahead was criss-crossed with small streams and pools of water.

In its formative years, the Couchsacrage was covered with glaciers, and when they melted, these massive rivers of ice had left erratics, large and small rocks and boulders from a distant land, scattered everywhere.

As Vasily surged forward, he found one, frozen in the ground right beside a backwater. He stubbed his toe, and his momentum carried him face first into the frigid pool. By the time he righted himself, and sat up, he was completely soaked. Not one item of clothing that he wore was dry.

The shock of the cold water took his breath away. He could feel a numbing current running under his belt, and as he stood up, it ran down both legs. It was cold, so cold, so icy cold.

His pack! Dry clothes in the pack! Oh, God no! Where is the pack? Why did he throw it away? To hell with the others! He had a stove, some food, a sleeping bag. He could curl up and wait for the storm to stop. He didn't need the others! Oh God! Where was the pack?

Now he ran aimlessly about. Pauly or the pack, he would settle for either one. He hoped that the running would warm him up. But in what direction? Where should he go?

But the Couchsacrage was too thick. There were too many obstacles. He couldn't maintain any speed in any direction. The low hanging branches gripped at him, and tried to pull him down. He would fight through an icy wall of coniferous needles, only to find broken trees and stumps, like some medieval fortification, blocking his way.

He gasped for breath; he needed to rest. He sat down, not caring where. The coldness began to wrap its chilly appendages around him. He began to shiver uncontrollably.

Feebly, he called for help once more.

Twice more he got up, and ran about, searching for something that could help him. Each time he got winded, and had to rest. Each time, the effort to move again seemed to demand more and more energy. He felt so cold, so hopelessly cold.

Finally, the will to go on ebbed away. Hypothermia, the deadly killer was upon him. He lay cold, exhausted, with visions of his homeland, and the warmth of the stove by the kitchen table.

And there he died.

Somewhere in the Couchsacrage.

Chapter 26

Mike was lying under the plane, his back supported by the side hill. He stared off into the rain and the mist.

Emotionally, it had been a fight for Mike. He feared that the lurching plane had done more damage to his injured spine, and his anger had been directed plainly and emphatically toward Angela.

He had been hired to watch over her and protect her, but it all seemed so long ago. Maybe in the other world she was the governor's coveted daughter, but at the moment he thought of her as a clutzy blonde.

Still, she seemed so genuinely remorseful. The more he thought about the situation, the more he embraced the initial premise: there were two survivors, and they needed to help each other until a rescue party could arrive. And nobody knew how long that would be.

With this in mind he subdued his animosity.

"What were you trying to do?" he asked.

His calmer voice soothed her to a degree, but anxiety still gripped her. She couldn't handle the thought that she may have injured him more severely.

She sighed, and a tear worked its way slowly down her cheek. "I wanted to cut that tree branch out of the window," she explained softly, "I wanted to cover the opening with a tarp, so we would be more comfortable inside. I didn't know that the branch was holding up that end of the plane."

He admired her grittiness. She had been raised in privilege, with advantages most youngsters did not have. One might expect that she would be acting like a poor little rich kid, but instead she appeared to be willing to do all she could to help them to survive.

He had watched her from afar during several political functions, and had at that time concluded that she was a bit too aloof for his taste. Now they were involved in an unfortunate circumstance that afforded him an opportunity to see her in a different light, and he had to admit that he was pleased by what he saw.

So he decided that, no matter what his physical prognosis turned out to be, even if her actions had caused him further injury, he would not hold a grudge against her for the rest of his life. Not at all.

Once again it was time to make the best of things.

"Okay," he said, "Let's get to work making an acceptable camp site. I can make suggestions, and I can do what I can to help with my hands. You'll have to do the rest."

She was glad to hear his upbeat tone. She wiped the tears off her cheeks.

"Let's do it!" she said.

He looked above his head, at the plane that seemed to hang dangerously above.

"I'd like to get out from underneath this thing," he said, "We need a tent or a lean-to or something. What did you do with the chain saw?"

Immediately she moved around the plane, to the high ground behind it. When she returned, she had the chain saw in her hands.

"I don't think the plane will move anymore," she reported. "It's still hung up in some branches, and the bottom is wedged against the side hill."

"Just the same, I'd like to be out from under it." He didn't sound like he trusted her judgment yet.

He selected two spruces near the plane site. They were tall enough, and straight, and about a tarp's width apart. In the sand he drew a picture of a cross pole wedged across their branches, about four feet from the ground, with a tarp tied across the middle. "We'll need to lash the pole in place," he explained, "and if we stake ropes to the ground to hold the tarp, it will keep the weather off. We can build a fireplace nearby."

She seemed to immediately grasp what needed to be done, and set to work right away, cleaning the lower branches from the spruces, and cutting a young beech to make the cross pole.

Meanwhile he cut and tied pieces of rope through various eyeholes of the tarp, so that it could be staked to the ground later.

The entertaining part came when she draped the tarp over the cross pole and attempted to climb one of the trees to set it in place. Each time she got half way up the tarp slid off the pole.

He watched eagerly to see how she would solve the problem. In his mind he wished for a body healthy enough to give her a hand. The two of them would have no trouble at all setting the tarp in place.

Although she seemed to be aggravated each time the tarp fell, she was willing to give it several tries. He thought he could hear her muttering under her breath.

Finally she tied a rope to the tarp to hold it in place while she climbed. With this adjustment she was able to get the cross pole and the tarp where they belonged. Then, using a large rock as a hammer, she staked down the ropes Mike had tied to hold the corners.

She turned to look at him with a big smile.

"Ta ta! I present to you the big top!" she cried.

Some of the knots she had tied looked a little crude, but the shelter seemed to be secured well enough.

It was a good ten yards from where Mike was to the new shelter.

"Are you sure that you want to move over here?" she asked. "Won't you hurt yourself more?"

He looked over his head to the plane that still hovered precariously over his head.

"I'd rather be crippled than crushed. Nobody knows what that damned thing is going to do," he reasoned. With that he began to pull himself with his arms across the ground to the new safer shelter.

It took some work to get him into a sleeping bag and onto an air mattress. But with this done she searched about for odds and ends to prop his head up, so he could see what was going on.

Then she busied herself collecting rocks from the side of the brook, and she fashioned a fireplace a short distance from the tarp.

"Once you get a fire going," he told her, "it will burn okay in this mist if you keep it hot enough."

She had no trouble finding firewood in the woods nearby. Years of blow down had strewn many dead branches about, and with the chain saw she could cut them into manageable pieces.

Still, the wood was very wet on the outside. Mike instructed her to crawl under the spruces for dry twigs, and to peel a couple of birches he could see. "You can cut some of those alders over there," he suggested, pointing to swampland that was upstream along the brook. "That darned stuff will burn anytime. Once you get some hot coals, you'll be all right."

After awhile she had a steady, but smoky, fire going. The radiant heat wasn't very effective, but the thing cheered up the environment considerably.

"Come nightfall we might want to move closer," she said.

"Or we can just pull some rocks from the side of the fire and snuggle next to them," he suggested.

"We can call them 'bed rocks'," she joked.

They both giggled at the silliness.

Once again she was in the plane, and returned with a small camp stove and some freeze dried food. In no time she was down by the stream collecting water in a pot.

"We'll eat well tonight," she announced cheerily, "Chef a la Angela!"

"Let me!" he insisted. "You've worked hard enough. I can work the stove. Just bring it to me."

Soon they were eating a meal that, considering the circumstances, did not taste bad at all.

Later, after she had washed the dishes, she sat down on the ground beside him.

"This is fun," she said. "I think after I'm married and have children, I'll take them on camping trips, whenever I can."

Chapter 27

Vitilli felt like he should congratulate himself. All things considered, they had made some progress.

By his map and by some seat-of-the-pants dead reckoning, he now determined that they were now traveling through the vast Hedgehog Swamp, and that a due south course might lead them to an area of concentric contour lines known as Hardwood Island. This area wasn't actually "an island," but it was a high ground in the marshland that could offer a relatively dry place to set up tents for the night.

Hardwood Island wasn't exactly along the compass course Vitilli wished to follow, but he'd seen enough of the swamp for the day. It would be dark in a couple of hours. They needed to settle in.

"This'll be worse than boy scouts," he muttered. "These damned fools don't know anything about camping. I'll have to nurse them along, all the way."

He would divide the crew into two groups. He would be in charge of three men, and he would appoint Woody, the only other experienced camper, in charge of the rest of the crew. Things should work out.

"Damned weather!" he complained, as the icy mist continued. In his heart, however, he hoped that the storm would continue until he got his men out of the Couchsacrage and to a safe haven.

The land began to rise now. Hardwood Island! Time to set up camp for the night. He picked a spot that seemed flat enough, and began to clear the ground of objects.

It was when the other men came up that he realized that someone was missing.

"Where the hell is Vasily? Where's Boris? Who the hell was next to him in the swamp? Where did he go?"

Vitilli paced back and forth like a caged lion.

Cowardly Pauly made no sound. He had known that Vasily had fallen behind hours ago. At first he had tried to hail Abdul, but when the strange dark man had not responded, he had shut up and continued on. If he had stayed sober, he thought, he might have been able to keep track of the lost comrade. It was all a muddle in his fried brain, and he didn't want to admit any responsibility.

It was MacIlwaine who responded. "He's gone, Bo. He's lost in that swamp somewhere."

Again the angry Vitilli queried, "Who was next to him in line?"

His eyes met Abdul's, who blankly stared back. This small act seemed to answer his question.

Pauly was relieved. He was afraid of Vitilli and his quick temper, but he knew that Bo would not mess with Abdul. Nobody in his right mind would.

Still, Vitilli raged at the group in general.

"Well, we've lost the food he was carrying and the cop's pistol that he had! And where the hell are we going to find another driver for his route? You guys have to watch out for each other in this godforsakin' place!"

He paced some more. "And he had a tent!" he continued, "and we ain't got enough tents now!"

After a short pause it was time for the concluding remarks: "Well, if the stupid son-of-a-bitch couldn't take care of himself...that oughtta be a lesson for all of you. Stick together!" Now that he had thought more about it, he had concluded that they could probably get along without Vasily.

"Maybe he will show up," the bland faced Martinson put in, stupidly.

Vitilli laughed sarcastically at this comment. "You idiot!" he sneered, "He's dead. This swamp kills! This weather kills!"

Then he turned to Woody. "Help Farley, Martinson, and Pauly set up camp." He looked at those three, "Who's got tents? Good, you have two. You guys can share tents and the grub you have. Mac and Abdul and I will camp over here," and with that he pointed to a spot on the ground.

"Let's move it," he shouted earnestly, "it will be dark soon. Let's get some food and get some sleep."

Later on, beside a sturdy cherry tree, Woody shared a tent with Martinson. His rifle was by his side, and he lovingly put his arm across it. "You'll be okay," he told his old friend, "you'll be okay."

He didn't like the way things were going. Visions of recent events raced through his mind. In the stolen sleeping bag he was warm and cozy enough, and the pit pat of the rain outside had a comforting and relaxing beat, but each time he closed his eyes he could see the frightened faces of Millie and Myron Arbur. Their eyes would haunt him until his dying day.

How could he get to sleep?

In the rain outside, in the pitch-blackness, an invisible figure rested against a beech tree. As the rain continued, he adjusted his poncho and stared ahead, as if there was something he could see.

Abdul would not share a tent with the others. He preferred to rest where he was.

Chapter 28

Although it was dry, and it offered a high ground above Neverending Swamp, the old railroad bed was now considerably less than a thoroughfare.

Too many years had passed. It was now covered with various types of vegetation, all tangled and grasping. The travelers no longer had to worry about holes and backwaters, but the clinging icy branches were still everywhere.

If fact, there were places that were so thick that the rescue party had to again descend briefly from the embankment and into the swamp in order to by-pass the obstruction.

Nevertheless, when darkness came, it offered a high and somewhat dry location for a decent campground. Two tents were quickly erected by Rose and Pete, and the party settled down in relative comfort.

Doc got the gas stove going, and Dag took charge of preparing a meal. The group ate ravenously. It had been a hard day, with very few stops, with a little gorp for nourishment at lunchtime. They were all very hungry.

The group did not talk much, to the relief of Rose, who worried that Dag and Pete would get into an argument again.

"You'll sleep with me," she said to Dag.

He considered it an honor to be invited to share a tent with this beautiful woman, but he realistically realized that she was merely keeping him and Pete apart.

One of the great comforts in life is to be warm and dry and snug in a sleeping bag in a waterproof tent, while one listened to the inclement weather beating a tap dance on the roof above. Dag stretched his body the length of his bag. He'd had a lot more exercise than usual today. He wondered how lame he would be in the morning.

"Good night, Dag," he heard Rose say.

"Where are you from, Rose?" Dag asked, "Where did you grow up?"

"I'm a Puerto Rican gal from the Bronx," she answered in the darkness, "I grew up in the shadow of Yankee Stadium."

"Well, you sure don't handle yourself like a city slicker," Dag put in, complimentarily, "it's a pleasure to be with such an accomplished outdoorsman. Or should I say, outdoors person?"

"You can call me what you want," she chuckled, "Name tags don't mean much to me. There are other more important things to be concerned about."

"Besides," she went on, "Once out of high school, I went into the army. I had a lot of training living out in the elements."

This revelation surprised Dag. "Don't take this wrong," he said after awhile, "but apparently I had you pegged for being younger than you are."

This caused her to laugh.

"Yep," she responded, "I'm afraid I'm a mite closer to your age than you thought. Anyway, what was Mrs. Dag like?"

"Well, my wife was very capable in the woods," he went on, his voice projecting both pride and loneliness. "We climbed the Adirondack forty-six high peaks together, and we fished and hunted and camped. We spent a lot of time here, along this road, going to and coming from our camp near Chub Pond."

"You really miss that place," Rose said.

He sighed. "We had over a dozen members, and we were just a bunch of fun loving, hard working slobs with no political clout at all. We didn't have a chance."

"Pete said the voters got their way."

"All I know is that when the state put up a bond issue to buy more land, the voters defeated it. Later they put up a bond to clean up Lake Champlain and Long Island Sound and the state's waterways, and a provision to buy land apparently was in there somewhere. It wasn't advertised. Very few people were aware of it. It was pretty sneaky."

"That's what you meant when you told Pete there was no democracy in it at all."

133

"Not the way I see it. I don't think the voters wanted to buy this land. Not at all."

"You have a right to be bitter, Dag," she sighed, "but we can't change all of that now. It's done, and we need some sleep."

"Good night, Rose," he said softly, "Thanks for listening and understanding."

Chapter 29

NEWS RELEASE (TV):

"Bernard Gordon with a WGHZ news bulletin.

"More news from the northeast ice storm, and the plight of New York State Governor Harry Bartholomew's daughter, Angela, who disappeared in the mists of the Adirondack State Park yesterday.

"No word has been yet received from the crash site. All radio contact seems to have been severed. Because of the current weather crisis, the only possible rescue effort at this point would have to be on foot, into the designated wilderness area known as The Couchsacrage.

"The site of the downed plane is known, and a rescue team of four individuals, led by D.E.C. Forest Ranger Pete Randolph and State Police Officer Rosemary Fernandez have entered the wilderness. They are accompanied by two volunteers.

"A recent call from Ranger Randolph indicates that they are presently bivouacked for the night. They are optimistic that they will reach the crash site tomorrow.

"The welfare of the three occupants of the plane is still unknown.

"More later. Please stay tuned."

Chapter 30

Call of nature.

Dag carefully and quietly slid from his sleeping bag and out of the tent. No need to awaken Rose.

He snapped on his flashlight. The storm allowed no moonlight, no starlight. There was no illumination at all near the campsite. Total blackness.

The sleet continued to form on the ground, as the tiny icy globules settled down from the sky. He reached back inside the tent for his boots. The ground was far too cold to be moving about barefoot.

In the distance, along the edge of the marsh he could hear the cracking and breaking of trees and branches. "What a mess this storm is leaving in its wake," he thought.

Quickly he went about his business; then he turned to head back into the tent. He didn't know the time, but he presumed that daybreak, or a gloomy substitute for it, would be happening in a few hours.

He heard a man cough. Somebody else was up and about. He waved his flashlight back and forth in order to see who it was.

Doc Ginsberg! Curled up in some alders right near him. The redness of the man's eyes indicated that he might have been crying!

"Jeepers, Doc," Dag said softly, "I almost peed on you. What's going on? You should be tucked away in your sleeping bag."

"Couldn't sleep," the volunteer E.M.T. answered brusquely. He seemed to be annoyed that anyone had found him there.

"Okay!" Dag exclaimed, himself a little vexed at Doc's attitude, "Sorry I'm alive!"

Then he turned to go back to his tent. "See you in the morning," he added.

"Wait!" Doc whispered. There was a hint of desperation there.

"What do you want, Doc?" Dag replied. He liked Doc Ginsberg. He would help if he could.

"I need therapy," was the answer.

"Just a moment," Dag responded. He was gone briefly to retrieve his raincoat from under the tent flaps. When he returned he said, "I'm no psychologist, you know."

"You're of the earth," Doc went on, "You're a man who knows the world. An Ivy League egghead I don't need. I want to talk to a friendly bartender."

"Wait right here," Dag said again. After a moment of rummaging through his pack, he returned once more. He sat on a log beside his friend, and aimed the beam of the flashlight at an icy spruce tree. The reflection from the whiteness provided some visibility to converse by.

"Back when we had a camp in here," Dag said, "We sat up and solved the problems of the world more than once. I guess we can pretend it's old times."

He handed Doc a bottle, and the medic took a swig. "I'll be damned," he said, "Yukon Jack!"

"Well, this is a hoary night," Dag said.

"Thanks," Doc replied, and took another small drink. "Good stuff!" he added.

Dag took a drink himself. "What the hell is going on, Doc?" he asked.

"I want to go back," Doc said.

"So do I," Dag agreed.

"No, you don't understand. I'm a poor choice for this job. I don't know if I can do it."

"But you're the best," Dag said sardonically. "This is an extreme emergency, and the Rangers needed an E.M.T. You were the only one in town. That makes you the best they could find. And now we are sitting in the depths of the Couchsacrage in the middle of the night getting wet and cold. You'll have to do the job!"

It was quiet for the moment. Dag feared that he had been a tad too jocular about the situation. It was apparent that Doc did not see the irony.

"Got a cigarette?" Doc's voice again.

"Nope." Got some small cigars though."

Dag produced two of them from his pocket, and handed one to his friend, igniting his lighter as he did.

After a few puffs, Doc began, "I just recently renewed my certification, and I'm not sure I should have. I haven't treated anyone for years. I don't know if I can. I have something you might call a mental block."

"You're still the best," Dag said, trying to make light of Doc's concern. "Besides, Rose and that cracker jack ranger are certified too. Maybe all you'll have to do is assist them. Besides, there might not be anything to do at all. The people that were on the plane might all be dead, or maybe they'll just need a band-aid. Who knows?"

Doc was quiet again. Dag didn't know if the conversation was over or not. In a way he hoped he could just finish his cigar and go back to bed.

Then Doc spoke once more. "I once was an M.D., and I was part of a peace corps operation in Africa. We were occupying a village that had just been raided by a nearby tribe. One of my friends was badly wounded. We could not move him."

Dag sat silently.

"More brutal thugs arrived, and I could hear them coming up the street toward our position. They killed everybody in sight, old people, mothers and their babies, little kids, everybody. I can still hear their terrible screams! It was barbaric."

"Man's inhumanity to man," Dag sighed, "I don't believe there will ever be an end to it."

"I was a coward," Doc whispered, contempt dripping from his voice. "I just ran as fast as I could to get clear of there."

"And your friend?"

"When the gang reached him, I could hear his screams as they tortured and killed him."

It was Dag's turn to be silent. He had to think a moment about what he had just heard.

"I have this theory," he finally offered, "never judge a man unless you have walked in his shoes. I wasn't there, but I can tell you this, I think I would have done exactly as you did."

"But my friend…"

"Look, Doc. You would have been killed too. Your friend would have known that. Do you think he would have wanted you to hang around and die for nothing?"

In the darkness Dag could see the orange tip of Doc's lighted cigar as he took another drag.

"I've relived that moment a thousand times," Doc went on, "The memory of it wakes me from a sound sleep, and if you could see me better now you would notice how badly my hands are shaking. I don't know if I could treat anybody or not."

"Why did you re-certify?" Dag asked, "In the back of your mind there has to be a reason."

"I got tired of the self-pity. I'm trying to get on with it. Maybe I can help somebody, and maybe I can't."

"This will be a good trial run," Dag assured him. "Sure as rain. No pun intended."

Doc was not in a joking mood. "I'll tell you one thing," he added, "I'll never desert anyone who needs me again. Never. Never."

"Let's get some sleep," Dag suggested.

Chapter 31

Vitilli's camp was a busy one indeed. No one seemed to want to lie down for long. The men simply were not going to adapt to the outdoor life very easily. A couple of stolen lanterns glowed through the grimness. There was no point in turning one off, because somebody always seemed to be up and about.

So it was a restless crew; and they took turns getting up and out of their tents, and pacing about all night.

It drove Vitilli wild. "Goddam it, go to bed!" he shouted more than once, each time to no avail.

At one point, he had dozed off, quite comfortably, but a loud cracking sound shook the ground near his head.

Outside the tent, Pauly, Farley, and Martinson began to shriek, and a huge birch tree plummeted to the ground, barely missing Vitilli's tent as it smashed into a hundred pieces. Luckily it struck no one, and no equipment was damaged. But it got everybody up, and the light from a half a dozen flashlights cut the darkness.

Except Abdul, who did not move from his position under his poncho. It was like he had no nerves at all.

Vitilli and MacIlwaine were also up, checking for any damage done by the fallen tree.

"Are we going to get out of here tomorrow?" a nervous Farley asked, a slight whine to his voice.

"Yeah!" Vitilli said, unsure of his answer. In truth, although he was quite sure where he was, he had no idea of how long it would take to traverse around all the unknown obstacles that would be in their path.

No one got much of a rest, and as the daylight began to brighten the grayness a bit, some were asleep and some were milling about.

One thing was apparent. The icy rain and the dark mists continued. No let up seemed to be in order for today.

MacIlwaine appointed himself breakfast cook for some, and Woody manned the other stove.

"Eat up, dammit," Vitilli ordered. "It's gonna be another long day."

Packing the muddy and wet gear was not easy. Experienced hikers have patience enough to deal with such a mess. These men didn't. Vitilli shook his head at the sorry packs he saw. Mud and ice everywhere.

He called a meeting.

"I heard some of you guys whining and bitching all night long," he began, "and I don't want to hear any more. Nobody said this was going to be easy.

"Use some common sense. If we hung around the cabin we'd be going to prison soon. For some of us it would be for a long, long time.

"Now I'm not sure I can get you to where I wanted, but I can get you out of this place. I don't know where, and probably the cops won't know where either. That's our ace in the hole. We'll work from there.

"If anybody wants out, if anybody wants to go it alone, you can go for it. But we only have one compass that I know of, and I'm keeping it."

It was Farley's squeaky voice again, "Nobody wants to end up like Boris!"

They all nodded at that, except Abdul, who kept staring straight ahead.

Woody was thinking of desertion. He would play along for a while, but if the sun came out so he could get some bearings, and he saw a chance to make a break for it, he planned on breaking free. It would be tricky. Vitilli and MacIlwaine worried greatly about witnesses. When Vitilli had said that anybody could leave if they wanted to, he was just shooting off his mouth. He didn't mean it for a moment. Woody would have to pick the right moment to disappear.

The lessons of yesterday had been lost on Pauly. He had already indulged in his morning dose of his favorite drug. Now he was ready to go.

Abdul glared at him. "You better be last in line," he warned. "If we lose another man, it will be you!"

A cold chill ran up Pauly's spine. It seemed obvious that Abdul knew what had happened yesterday!

Vitilli had a new strategy. He would use the compass to cross the swamp at its narrowest, and try to escape from the Couchsacrage on higher ground. He was sick of all of the branches and roots and waterholes.

But it was still a long way from here to there, and in a mist so thick that they could only see a few feet ahead, they soon were all back among the alders, dealing with mud and water and thick icy vegetation. The aimless meanderings continued.

Vitilli studied his ancient map again and again. He noticed that somewhere in their vicinity there had once been a railroad line. He wondered if any semblance of that ancient structure still remained.

He looked at the holes and rivulets before him. "Helluva place for a railroad track," he mumbled.

It was fodder for a new effort. He liked the more immediate goal of finding some easier passage.

Two hours later, Martinson shouted out. "Bo! Bo! There's a rise in the ground ahead. Looks like some kind of winding ridge…"

"Check it out!" Vitilli ordered.

"I don't want to leave the group," Martinson answered tremulously.

"We're not going anywhere; we'll be right here," Vitilli assured him.

Martinson cautiously edged away from his place in line, looking back several times to be sure that no one was leaving him. He was moving so slowly that Vitilli lost his patience.

"Woody! For chrissakes, go with him," he ordered. "Goddam wimp needs somebody to hold his hand."

The mists would come and go, subject to any zephyr that came along. At times Vitilli's men could see their two comrades, and then a white curtain would block their view. With nowhere else to go, everybody stayed put.

"Hey! C'mon over!" shouted Martinson suddenly. His voice carried an amount of enthusiasm. "It's an old road, I think. It seems to go on and on!"

Vitilli led the others to the structure, and up the steep bank they climbed.

MacIlwaine noticed the edge of a huge block of wood sticking up in the air.

"It's an old railroad tie!" Vitilli announced gleefully. "We can follow this damned thing out of here!"

The others were also feeling a sense of guarded optimism. Most took a break and sat on a rock or a bent tree. It was time for a rest.

Vitilli dragged his map out again. The old railroad had many spurs, and each weaved confusingly about. He was on one of these old byways, but he had no clue which way to go. Where would they come out?

He shrugged his shoulders. One way would be as good as another. As far as this structure was concerned he was as lost as anybody else.

This he would keep to himself.

Chapter 32

There is nothing like breakfast on the trail, particularly if it is modified by frozen rain and the chill of the mist.

"My favorite!" Dag exclaimed, showing a lack of genuine enthusiasm for the formless glop staring back from his aluminum plate.

"Well," Rose smiled. "I have instant orange drink, cold biscuits, a little strawberry preserves, and instant coffee! I even heated the water myself with my own little camp stove!"

With that each member of the rescue party was gulping down what they had prepared.

It was barely dawn. But there was enough light so that, even before breakfast had been prepared, most of the packs had been stuffed with wet soggy equipment.

"It was a pleasure sharing a tent with you," Dag said sweetly, and he raised his cup as a gesture of respect.

"Thank you," Rose nodded. "Actually I love the company of older men."

"Older?" he cried, in mock disbelief that she would refer to him that way. Then he smiled and said, "I accept the tribute in the spirit given."

She sensed that he might have taken her remark the wrong way. Certainly she would not want to hurt Dag's feelings. "I'm serious," she said sincerely, "My dad was several years older than my mother."

"Well," he asked grudgingly, "Do I remind you of your father?"

She smiled sweetly, "Only in the sense that you would make a girl a nice husband."

His face brightened. "Nice compliment," he said.

"I always liked movies where the heroes were older men," she added. "My mom showed me some DVDs where Sean Connery was the hero, you know, in some of his later movies. I thought he was the sexiest man alive!"

Dag chuckled. "Well, that's the movies. In reality I think that a man who is my age should be careful about being with younger women. We couldn't even want the same things."

"Like what?" she asked in a teasing tone.

"Rest. Relaxation. Peace and quiet."

"I like that too."

"A woman like you would want to go, go, go. All of that would tire me out."

"Well, we're on the go here. You're holding your own."

"I'll get tired before you will."

"I may be a short-term sprinter. You're more like the marathon man."

"Children! All women want children."

She sighed. There was a secret there where she wasn't sure she wanted to go quite yet, but he had broached the subject.

"I have two children, a boy and a girl, "she confessed. "They are with my mother in the city. I can't do this job and have them to watch over."

Dag could see that she didn't want the conversation to go in this direction any further.

The whole conversation was perplexing, as far as Dag was concerned. By rights he should be having a paternal relationship with this lady. But things didn't seem to be drifting in that direction. What was going on?

Feeling somewhat exasperated and wanting to lighten up the conversation, he said, "C'mon, what about all the young handsome studs on TV and in the movies?"

"Too immature," she replied, relieved that he wasn't going to interrogate her about her past. "Experience is much better."

"Well, I hope you find the right guy for you," he replied, "He'll be a lucky man, I'll tell you that."

She gave him her brightest smile yet.

He marveled at how pretty she was, in spite of her garb, and the precipitation running down her face.

"Thank you for such a sweet compliment," she said.

At that moment, Pete was impatiently tying the last article to his pack. It was time to pick up and move out. As they stood up, icy water that had been accumulating in puddles on their ponchos splashed to the ground.

Dag smiled ironically. Imagine having a romantic conversation in the middle of such a miserable storm? He shook his head in befuddlement. Rose had certainly given him something to think about.

"Well," he muttered to himself, "a fantasy certainly will help pass the time as we trek along."

He shrugged his shoulders and stepped into line behind Pete.

As the ice pellets came down, and trees crashed in the distance, the little party was once again on the move.

Chapter 33

Angela was pretty content. "Roughing it" had a certain appeal to it.

"You like this stuff, don't you?" was Mike's question, as he watched her pile wood. She had been coming and going all morning.

The stuff she was forced to wear sure looked big on her. She looked like a ball of used laundry, and Mike thought her appearance was quite comical.

She stopped to roll up a long pant leg once more.

"I always wanted to sleep under the stars," she replied, "like the cowboys."

Then she looked upward, at the grimness of the mist and the ever present falling rain. "But there ain't no stars here, partner."

"When there are stars, help will be here," Mike said hopefully.

Cheerfully she bounced over toward him, a happy smile on her face. "I wonder where we are," she pondered. "Do you have any idea?"

"I think so," Mike replied. "See those rocks over there? Gneissic. A form of metamorphosed granite."

"What are you, a geologist?"

He laughed. "Hey, I was a Social Studies major. I loved my geology classes. Geology explains a lot about where people live and what they do for a living."

"Well, nobody lives here!" Angela observed.

"Maybe they used to. I was staring down the brook while you were gathering wood. Sometimes the mist will clear just a little, and you can see a bit farther. I think there is an old culvert down there, below a rock ledge that sticks out. And the culvert is buried under hundreds of rocks, almost as if they had been set there by hand, to keep the thing from washing away.

"Check it out. It's only a hundred feet or so from here,"

Angela was gone for a few minutes. When she returned she said, "It looks like there used to be a road there."

Mike brightened considerably. "The Couchsacrage!" he declared, "I think we're somewhere in the Couchsacrage!"

"Where?"

"I was thinking of our flight plan, and the speed we were going, and how far we had traveled before we went down. Yes, it makes sense, considering the geology and all, and now the old road. We're probably somewhere in the Couchsacrage."

"How do you say that? What does it mean?"

He laughed. "Dismal wilderness."

It didn't look like she cared for the translation.

Mike went on. "It's a large tract of state owned land within the Adirondack Park. Early settlers lumbered in here. Nearby towns had lumber mills, and later hunting camps and snowmobile trails…"

"People crossed through here a lot?"

"Well, now it's closed. Only people who would want to walk a long way through flat featureless swampland would come in here." Then he added sadly, "I guess I cheated, I'm in here and I can't walk at all."

She ignored his bitter comment. "It must be great for animals, like deer."

"Nah. Once it was closed to loggers, the forest grew up, and the food supply went down. The deer, for the most part, left. We're back to the days when the Iroquois and the Algonquins avoided this place. It is not a happy hunting ground."

"Well, lucky for us, we have available food," she said, changing the subject. "For lunch we have this funny mixture of candy and cereal and nuts and raisins…"

"It's called gorp," he laughed.

"And I can make some hot chocolate," she went on. "I have a pot near the fire, see? Instant hot water. All the modern conveniences."

For a while they sat quietly, munching on their treats and watching the fire.

Angela wasn't sure why, but she had already become accustomed to snuggling up next to him while they sat. Perhaps she needed a little assurance. She was very happy that she wasn't alone. Besides, it was warmer this way.

After awhile he asked, "What's it like being the governor's daughter?"

"Pretty boring. Too many functions to go to. I usually hate being there. I'm like a piece of furniture. I wish I could live a normal life like you."

"Well," he said, "I'm just an average guy, fresh out of college, looking for some direction."

"That's normal," she replied. "Most people go through that. My life is more structured. I don't control it, and I don't like it."

"That won't last forever,"

"Don't be too sure. Dad's now talking about running for President. There I'll be, on television, waving and smiling at a bunch of cheering people…"

Her voice got quieter, as if she was contemplating something. "I'll tell you this, Mike, when you see me like that, I'll be wishing that I was here, in the quiet forest, like we are now."

Her candor surprised him. He didn't know any way to respond to what she had just said.

"But if he wins, surely you can get away some of the time," he replied.

"Sure, with secret service agents following me everywhere. I'd like a more normal existence. I'm really just a regular gal."

He sighed. "You're a helluva lot more impressive than that. You would stand out even without your father's help."

She was thrilled by his observation. "Thank you!" she whispered, and gave him a little kiss on the cheek.

Back to reality. "Maybe I've crippled you for life," she said.

"Maybe the damage was done already," he said blandly, "Who knows?"

She was silent again, in a thoughtful mode.

"I have an idea," she said, finally.

"Yes?"

"I'll hire you for my permanent body guard. At least we can go through all of that baloney together."

"Me? A bodyguard? Like this?"

"C'mon," she protested, "Be positive! It's not certain that you won't recover. Have you seen your X-Rays? What did the experts say?"

She looked at him hopefully, sincerely. She secretly prayed for him to recover.

Then she added, in a more cheerful vein, "And besides, in the worst possible scenario, they can't refuse you employment because of a little disability."

He laughed. "You are a pistol!" he declared.

With that she stood up, and headed for the plane. "I might as well poke around some more," she announced. "Lord knows what Pilot Marks had stashed away."

157

"We could use some booze," he remarked, half-joking.

She returned momentarily.

"Look what I found!"

It was a bottle of bourbon. His wish had been granted.

She rustled up a couple of cups.

"I'm not really a drinking person," she announced, "but we should try a small taste. This is, after all, an emergency, and we should try to relax a little."

"We'd better ration it," Mike suggested. "We don't know how long we'll be here."

"Oh, there's more. A whole case of it!"

They sat and relaxed for a while, and watched little icy streams drip from various wrinkles in the tarp above. It was interesting to see how far the water would run along the ground before it froze.

When it got to be mid-afternoon, Angela asked, "When we get out of here, when we are home safe and sound, will you call me?"

Chapter 34

It was like seeing an old friend again!

To the others, it was an old rusty post. But to Dag, it triggered a wealth of old memories.

"Our club gate was here!" he announced, "We always stopped here for a beer on our way to camp."

Then he looked at Pete and his smile faded. "I guess you really don't care about that."

"I guess not," Pete said, matter-of-factly.

Dag glared at him, but he refrained from what he wanted to say. He had promised Rose that he would not argue with the ranger.

Still, Dag removed his pack from his back. "Time for a break," he said.

Pete was stern. "We haven't found them yet," he reminded the members of the party.

"You know," Dag put in, "I know where that plane is. It's farther than you think. We can rest here and have some semblance of energy when we get there, or we can rush and get more and more tired."

Pete turned to Rose, but he could see that she and Doc had already set their packs on the ground. He refused to let go of the notion that they should rush on ahead, and it annoyed him to see that Dag was casually lighting up a cigar.

"Exactly where do you think the plane is?" he queried. It seemed to him that Dag was pretty sure of himself.

"I saw the longitude and latitude that you had written down," Dag smiled annoyingly. "The plane is near the culvert at the base of Polecat Swamp. We've got a couple of miles to go yet."

"Can you find it?"

Dag looked at the ranger in disbelief. There was no point in answering the question. He doubted that he could do so without being sarcastic.

"Why don't you just sit here and enjoy a cigar, like I am. Why are you so up tight all the time?" Dag asked. With that he flipped open the top of his pack, to reach for his cigars once more.

"I don't smoke," Pete was saying, "I never picked up the filthy habit."

Dag shrugged. "Want one, Doc?" he asked, and the medic rose to retrieve Dag's offering.

Pete sighed. There was a log next to Dag's pack, and with considerable resignation, he sat down on it. It was simply by chance that he looked down into the pack at the time the Adirondacker returned his box of cigars.

To Pete's utter surprise he could see a holster, and a small pistol, placed carefully at the very top.

"You got a permit for that?" he asked.

Dag nodded perfunctorily. "Yes I do."

"Is it registered with the Bureau of Alcohol, Tobacco, and Firearms, like the recent legislation requires?"

"What? The cigars?" Dag couldn't help himself.

Rose and Doc could barely stifle their amusement.

"No dammit, the pistol!" Pete shouted in earnest.

Dag grabbed the case and lifted it from the pack. He held it so that the ranger, and everyone else could see.

"This is an antique. It's been handed down from generation to generation. They don't make pistols like this anymore."

"Is it registered?" Pete continued.

Dag's face flared with anger. "No, it's not! Guys like you took our camp, but you're not going to come and get my pistol!"

"I should confiscate it!" Pete declared.

"What are you, a game warden now? You think I'm going to shoot some deer that isn't here?"

"That gun is illegal!"

"Well, I'm keeping it. Don't you touch it. It is not a Saturday night special."

"Why did you bring it?"

161

"Why did you and Rose bring yours? It's here if we need it. Maybe a rabid raccoon, or something raiding our camp ground, or our rations could be damaged or lost and we need to shoot a rabbit...," then Dag couldn't help one more joke, "Maybe we'll run into some gangsters!" and he showed Pete his wild look.

Pete did not smile. "The law clearly states..."

"Good Lord! This is Rose's department, not yours!"

Pete looked back at Rose. His face was red, and he wanted her support.

Rose stepped forward, and addressed Dag directly, in an official, formal tone of voice. Dag did not care for her intonation.

"Ranger Randolph and myself are required by certain uniform codes to carry our pistols on a mission such as this. Why we've had to carry these heavy weapons into the Couchsacrage is beyond me, but they are here in case we might confront an emergency situation where they might be useful. I don't know why anybody else would burden themselves this way."

Pete seemed to be satisfied by the way she was handling it so far. Doc was mesmerized by the sudden conflict.

Dag's face reddened. So far he had gotten on very well with the lady trooper. But she wasn't going to take his gun either. He would quit the mission right here and now.

Rose had an amused look on her face as she went on.

"I hereby deputize Mr. Dagonneault, and I order him to be like us, and carry a useless piece of iron with him for the duration of the trip," she announced officially. "Once we return to civilization," she went on, "as a representative of New York State, I will personally help Mr. Dagonneault to take care of the much delayed paper work, so that he may legally maintain possession of the aforementioned collector's item."

Pete Randolph made a grab for his back pack and angrily put it on.

Then he turned to Dag and barked, "Show us the way to Polecat Swamp."

Chapter 35

The discovery of the railroad bed should have made Vitilli's task all the easier. It was no longer necessary to weave about in the dense swamp, searching for a place they could walk.

The compass had been put away. They were now committed to go wherever the road led them. Vitilli could only hope that when they reached a main highway somewhere, he could sort out where they were and act accordingly.

His worries were now being added to by the men themselves. Since the danger of anybody getting lost was gone, there was a lot of straggling going on. He could not convince them of the urgency of leaving the swamp. When he looked back they were spread all over the place. In fact, he couldn't see some of them at all. Where Martinson and Farley and Pauly were was a mystery.

He stopped for a cigarette.

The rains continued to drizzle on down. He looked at the sky and hoped it would all continue. He needed this storm in the worst way.

They most certainly would need to be out of the Couchsacrage by the time the sun came out.

Conflicts in his thinking arose. He and MacIlwaine and a few others could move on ahead, and escape the swamp, leaving the stragglers behind. But what if they were captured and they testified against Cheese's organization? What if they told about the murders? Four of the gang had committed no other crimes except robbery and drug running, certainly not capital offenses.

It was all very complex. He could wait for them, and act as a mother hen to get them through, or he could move on out, taking only those who could keep up. If he did the latter, he feared, he would have to kill some of them. That was for sure.

Goddam! If they would only keep up.

To make matters worse, the old map he had did not include all of the Couchsacrage. They were now in a corner which was unknown to him. This fact concerned him greatly. He hoped to find some way to get his bearings again.

And what if the sky cleared, and they weren't out of the swamp yet? What if the main highways were cleared, and cops were out on patrols at every trail head, waiting for them to appear? What then?

It seemed to him that his initial plan had been sound. There really hadn't been much of a choice there. But things had not gone as planned, and he was now very perplexed and worried.

"What if we had some hostages?" he thought. "We might be able to bargain our way to freedom."

It was a ridiculous notion. Where were they going to find hostages deep in the Couchsacrage?

"Goddam it! Move your asses!" he mumbled, as he looked back through the mist, trying to see his pokey comrades. There was no point in screaming at them. They were going to lollygag along at their own pace, no matter what.

Maybe it was because of the lack of sleep. Maybe that's why they moved so slowly.

Four men were up near the front of the line. Vitilli, MacIlwaine, Abdul, and Woody. They would have to sit and wait for the others to catch up.

It was MacIlwaine who noticed it first.

"Bo. Don't you smell smoke? It's almost like there is a camp fire near here."

Chapter 36

Mike was taking a nap.

Angela studied his face as he slept. Her mind looked back in time to the recent functions they had attended together. He had been just another guy who had been hired to watch over her. In time he would have been like the rest, and moved on to another job. She would have never gotten to know him, that was for certain.

She thought of the other escorts she'd had. Were they fine men, like Mike? She had barely ever spoken to any of them. She regretted her haughtiness. She had learned a lesson here. From now on she would try to get to know the people who surrounded her better.

There was something about the badly injured man who slept near the camp fire. It was like she never wanted to say "good bye" to him.

She had gathered some balsam branches. Mike had described them to her, and she had eagerly searched by the brook for them. They had such a wonderful smell. She tucked various cut branches under the sides of their air mattresses. "We can smell them as we fall asleep," she thought.

Out of the corner of her eye, she thought she saw some movement. The mist had parted down by the culvert ever so briefly, and it almost looked like someone had been standing there.

"A rescue party?" For Mike's sake she hoped that it was true.

Then again, it could be an animal. She shuddered at the thought. They had no weapons to fend off any intruders.

She studied the spot attentively.

Yes! There is a man there, and he's heading this way!

She was overjoyed. Help had come. She was surprised how soon they had arrived. She was sure her heart would burst because of the excitement she felt.

Her sense of relief would be quashed in very short order.

A short, stocky, swarthy man led several others. She could not tell how many there were. They didn't seem to have any official uniform or anything. One man, a younger one, had a rifle strapped to his back. It was all very strange.

"Hello, there!" the short man was saying. He was already studying the downed plane. "Looks like there's been an accident here. Is everybody all right."

The comment alarmed her. Surely a rescue party would be expecting to find a plane. This man seemed to be surprised at what he saw.

"Hi, I'm Angela," she said in her most friendly voice. "We're the two survivors, and my friend here is badly hurt."

"I'm Bo," the man said. "This is Mac, and Woody, and Abdul. We hope we can help."

His bogus friendliness did not fool her. The other men had already spread out, and the one he had called Abdul had drawn a pistol. This was very frightening. Already a queasy feeling began to grip her. These people were not here to help.

Another man was arriving! How many were there? This particular man was short and stocky and grubby.

"Hey, Farley, glad you could make it," the man called Bo said, sarcastically.

Right away Farley noticed Angela, and he moved to her side. A grin exposed yellow, poorly kept teeth. "Wow, Bo," he snickered, "It looks like we've found us a cutie."

"You better watch out when her boy friend wakes up," MacIlwaine joked, and Farley moved away from her. His genuine caution made the rest chuckle.

Two other men arrived. One had a half-smile, like he was enjoying a private joke. The other was tall, bewhiskered, and ugly.

"Finally," Vitilli remarked, "We're all here. Pauly, Martinson, Farley…climb into the plane and see what's here. Look especially for a radio or a phone. I'm not sure we want any communication with the outside world."

The three thugs moved immediately to do as they were ordered.

Alden L. Dumas

That did it as far as Angela was concerned. This was not a group of people she wanted to be dealing with.

"Who are you people?" she demanded.

"Hikers!" Vitilli joked derisively. "Enjoying the great outdoors."

"Hey, Bo!" Pauly shouted from the plane, "There's a stiff up here in the pilot's seat, with half a head. He ain't going no where." Then he yelled, "Hey, Abdul, it looks like one of your jobs!"

"And the radio's smashed all to hell," Martinson added.

"Good," Vitilli answered.

He turned to Angela once again, flashing his sickening smile. "Is there anybody else in your party?"

Too many witnesses, he thought. They didn't need any more.

She gritted her teeth. What was to come of all of this?

"Nobody else," she reported flatly.

"And what's the matter with wonder boy here?" the little man wanted to know.

"His back. Maybe broken. He can't help you, and he can't hurt you," she said apprehensively.

He ignored her tone. Already he had pretty much lost interest in the injured man.

By now Pauly had dropped back down to the ground from the wreckage. He was wearing a nightgown, no doubt taken from Angela's suitcase.

"How do I look?" he grinned, and several of the others laughed at his appearance.

He looked evilly at Angela. "I'd like to see what she looks like in this. Pretty nice, I'll bet."

At this point, the young man named Woody stood up, his rifle still strapped to his back. "For chrissakes, Pauly," he lectured. "Have a little dignity." He had no use for Pauly, that was certain.

"Oh, ease up, Woody!" MacIlwaine warned. He didn't care much for Pauly's actions either, but he was more concerned about dissension.

Mike had awakened a while ago, and had quietly been observing the invaders. Like, Angela, he was very alarmed at what he saw. He particularly didn't like the three men who were nosing about everything.

"Please leave our personal stuff alone," he asked.

Pauly sidled up near him. "Oh, shut the hell up, cripple boy," he warned.

Mike looked to the men he thought might be the leaders, but they seemed to ignore Pauly and the others, and let them do as they liked.

"Hey! Look what I found!" Farley was lowering himself from the plane now, carrying a large carton. "Whiskey! Bourbon! It looks like a party tonight!"

Vitilli rolled his eyes. If he'd had trouble moving this crowd up to now, it didn't look like things were going to get any easier.

"At least wait until you've set up your tents and got some food out," he lectured. He gave up thinking of traveling any more on this day. He prayed that the storm would continue for a while yet.

Martinson was now by his side.

"Read this, Bo!" he said, excitement in his voice.

Vitilli took the paper in his hand. It was a letter, to be delivered to some official in Quebec. There was an identification card, with a picture.

"Well, well, well!" he announced. "Do you know who we have here?"

All activity stopped. All eyes were on him. He turned to Angela.

"So you're the governor's daughter!" he announced loudly, contemptuously. "We have a celebrity in our midst. Better yet, boys, we have ourselves a perfect hostage if we need one."

He couldn't believe his good fortune.

MacIlwaine wasn't so sure. "Bo," he warned, "this plane is a magnet. As we speak, there has to be a rescue party headed this way. We'd better be on the look out."

Chapter 37

"Chub Pond," Dag cried, pointing to the right.

It was a small pond, as Adirondack ponds go, merely a kettle formed from an ice block during glacial times. Still, the mist obliterated the view of the other side.

"We might as well be on the shore of the Pacific Ocean," Doc reflected.

"How far now?" Rose asked.

"Not far," Dag assured her.

"Well, I want to rest a moment," Rose said. She knew that Pete would object, but she didn't care. "When we hit that crash site there might be lots to do. A couple of moments of rest here will better enable us to do what we will need to do when we get there."

"I agree," Doc said. He continued to worry about what his role would be.

Dag was looking at the pond.

"It's like seeing paradise," he reminisced. "Over there, on a nice day, you could see a big rock where we used to sit and catch bull heads by the pailful. Sometimes we would be here almost all night long. Then we'd go back to camp, all tired and happy."

"What did you do with them all?" Rose asked.

"Those darned things seem to live for hours and hours. When we'd wake up the next morning most of them would still be alive. It would take us hours to clean them. At night we would have a wonderful meal."

"Are they that good to eat?" Rose asked.

"My goodness yes," Dag went on, "All breaded and fried. Nothing better."

"And what did you do with the leftovers?" Pete asked.

Dag took a deep breath, and fought for composure. Even though there was no limit on the number of bullheads they could catch, this guy still wanted to see if they wasted anything.

"We would take them back to town to our grandparents," Dag assured him. "They were very happy to get them. We were very good boys."

"Well," Pete said stiffly, "The state bought this land so everybody could enjoy the experience, not just a chosen few."

"And they really succeeded didn't they," Dag shot back angrily. "Nobody has fished this pond for years. When they closed the road no one came here any more!"

Pete's face reddened, and his composure stiffened.

"It's hard to feel sorry for you people," he declared. "Almost all of the leases were for short terms, and everybody knew that they could be terminated at any time."

"Listen to yourself!" Dag shot back. "If you're at the funeral of a good friend, what do you tell his children and his grandchildren? 'It's hard to feel sorry for you. You knew all the time that the old boy would die eventually'?"

Pete stood up abruptly. "This land has to be protected from polluters, developers...," he raged.

"And I agree with you there!" Dag interrupted.

"Stop! Stop! Stop!" Rose suddenly shouted. "Finally you both agree on a point! Let it rest there!"

She glared at both men. Then she angrily grabbed her pack and began to put it on.

"Let's go!" she commanded, petulantly.

Surprisingly, Pete helped Dag with his pack.

"Obviously we have severe philosophical differences here," he acknowledged. "Maybe we'll never see eye to eye."

Pete's amicable gesture surprised Dag, and encouraged him to take a lighter stance as well.

"Dammit, Pete, I don't want to fight with you. I know you believe devoutly in protecting this land. But if you didn't grow up here, if you didn't know the joy we felt while we shared this wilderness, how could you possibly know how I feel? How could you understand the despair and exasperation we felt when we had to leave for good?"

Chapter 38

In a while they came to a steep rock outcrop overhanging what once was the road.

"Stanley's Peak," Dag said. "An old friend killed several deer from here. If you left the road here, and dropped down the hill behind this rock ledge, you would soon be deep into Polecat Swamp."

A few hundred feet from Stanley's Peak they came across a fork in the road. It was now grown up pretty badly, but it was still recognizable. Dag stopped and pointed to the right.

"Go down the hill there," he said, "and you'll come to the brook that drains Polecat Swamp. There should be an old culvert there. Go upstream, and almost immediately you will come to the plane."

"Aren't you going?" Rose asked.

"I'll be right along," Dag said quietly. "I want to visit a few ghosts first."

So with Pete in the lead, the three descended the hill. Sure enough, when they reached the culvert, the acrid smell of a campfire was very apparent.

Pete and Rose both wanted to rush now. They had reached their goal and were anxious to get busy with whatever their duties might be. They had no reason to think they needed to be cautious here.

When they could see the campfire they noticed three people. Rose breathed a sigh of relief. Three survivors! Wonderful!

The assuagement was brief. No sooner had they rushed into camp when they were surrounded by men, and two of them held pistols. There was a tall, dignified looking man under the wing of the plane, and another, with dark threatening eyes, under a tree by the fire.

"We've been expecting you," Vitilli said sweetly, "Now, take off your packs and stay awhile."

"And take their pistols," MacIlwaine ordered. "They will not need them."

"Woody, Farley," Vitilli added. "You now each have a weapon to be in charge of. Use them carefully."

Farley was all too eager to remove the pistol from the policewoman. His wandering hands revolted her as he followed his orders. He looked at her with a sickening grin.

On the other hand, Pete sensed that the man who disarmed him wasn't entirely eager to do so. But he disregarded the feeling. Maybe it was just his imagination.

"Is this other guy armed?" Martinson inquired, looking at Doc.

"He's a medic," Rose informed him. "He can help anybody who is hurt."

"Thank God," the blonde girl near the fire blurted.

To appease her, Vitilli nodded toward Mike. "Take care of him," he said. Might as well keep the girl happy for now.

Doc kneeled by the injured man's side.

"I think you're too late," Mike said rancorously. "my back is broken."

"We'll see," Doc said quietly. "I have some tests we can try. Can somebody help me get this lad out of the sleeping bag?"

Angela was there immediately to help, but the others would not move.

"Can we help?" Rose asked Vitilli, while she stared at the barrel of Abdul's gun.

"You can," Vitilli answered, "but ranger boy here has to answer some questions."

While the small group tried to help Mike, Abdul watched suspiciously. There had better not be any funny stuff.

"What's going on?" Pete asked.

"Sorry about all of this," Vitilli went on. "Unfortunately, you are here. And we are here. It's all very inconvenient."

"Who are you? Why are you here?" Pete wanted to know.

Vitilli smiled. "I'll ask the questions. Are there just three of you?"

179

"Yes," Pete lied. He immediately sensed the danger at hand and that it might be of some value if these thugs didn't know about Dag. He hoped that Rose and Doc were listening, and would stick to the same story, if asked.

He took a quick glance at Rose. She nodded subtly. He took that to mean she was tuned in.

"Any other rescue parties on the way?"

"Yes!" Another lie. "I heard one was leaving early today. They could be arriving soon."

"Screw this!" an agitated Pauly blurted. "Let's kill them all and get the hell out of here!"

The outburst stunned all of the prisoners.

"No!" MacIlwaine protested. "If anybody else is within earshot, gun fire will warn them. We need the element of surprise."

He looked back over his shoulder at the path behind them.

"Besides, we have plenty of hostages now," Vitilli added.

"Yeah," Farley squealed. "We got the governor's daughter and a lady cop. How much better can it get?"

"The rest can keep until we're ready to leave." MacIlwaine opined, "It'll be better to draw attention to this spot while we're heading for somewhere else."

"Farley, Martinson," Vitilli ordered, "Take the cop and the ranger and find a place to tie them up. See that stump down by the brook? That'll be a good place."

"It's plenty wet down there," Pauly giggled. "It ain't out of the elements."

"We'll let them wear their jackets, and we'll let them keep their ponchos," MacIlwaine sighed patiently. He was a cold-blooded killer, but putting prisoners through unnecessary discomfort was something he would not be a party to.

He could tell by their expressions, that Pauly and Farley did not want to make the accommodations.

"Do what you're told," Mac said, in a cold tone.

Soon Rose and Pete were bound to the log by the brook, and their jacket and panchos were in place as MacIlwaine had ordered.

In a minute, though, Farley, Pauly, and Martinson were at it again, this time dumping the visitor's packs all over the ground. Clothes, personal effects, equipment, were all strewn everywhere.

In disgust Rose noted that Pauly and Farley were holding up some of her undergarments, and looking her way, with sickening smirks on their faces.

"Look," Martinson said, "Radios. Bet you could call anywhere!"

"Get rid of them." Vitilli ordered. "Make sure they won't work!"

Martinson took aim at a rock in the forest. In turn each radio pinged off it and into the swamp.

"We don't need anybody to call for help." Vitilli added.

"What about the phones on their belts?" Pauly asked, "What about them?"

"Get 'em." Vitilli ordered. "Wait, I've got an idea. Get the phones, and untie the ranger boy and bring him back up here."

Then he turned to Martinson, and with a nod toward Angela, he said, "Bring Goldilocks over here."

Pete was soon beside him once more, with MacIlwaine's pistol trained on his head.

Next to them was Angela, held tightly by the arm by Martinson.

Vitilli took one of the phones and handed it to Pete. Then he took his pistol and held it against Angela's mouth. He grabbed her arm, and twisted it roughly behind her. The expression in her eyes reflected the terror she felt.

He seemed to be enjoying all of this just a little too much.

"I know that you have to call in to command base," he began, "and it's time for you to call. Now, you tell them that you're here, and everything is fine, and everybody is good and healthy. You tell them that there is no need to rush in here, and to call off any other rescue party that is on the way. All the cops and rangers need to do is sit tight until the weather clears, everything will be fine."

As Angela and Mike had found earlier, the phone would not work at the plane crash site. This meant that Vitilli and a few of his grungy cohorts had to roughly escort Pete and Angela to the culvert and off toward Baldy Peak Hill. Eventually they found a spot where the call could be made.

Chapter 39

Dag felt relieved. As far as he was concerned, he had done his share.

In a little while, he would descend the hill and join his fellow rescuers, and he was sure that already they were at work taking care of what needed to be done.

Pete or Rose will radio on to their command headquarters, and give the status report. Then they will do whatever they can to make any victims comfortable. In a few days, when the weather clears, a rescue helicopter will arrive, and everybody will be shuttled out of here.

End of story.

The trip in to his old hunting grounds had been emotionally painful. Too many memories of great times that had come and gone raced through his mind. The gate post, Chub Pond, the railroad bed itself, even particular knolls and valleys and rocks, jarred loose thoughts that had been buried for years. In a way he was thankful for the continuing rain and mist, lest he be forced to look at more.

Still, out of respect, he had to return to where the camp had been one more time.

The site of the old camp was a mere fifty yards from the abandoned byway that led to the Polecat Swamp culvert. Slowly, reverently, he walked down the remnants of the old road. In a few seconds, he was there.

The camp had burned long ago, but the fire place, and its chimney, made of sturdy Adirondack rock, stood there as proudly as ever: a lone sentinel bearing testimony to times past.

He stood and looked at the site for what seemed to be a long time. He could almost see the visage of old Marvin, out in the morning splitting kindling. There he was, a gob of chewing tobacco jutting from his cheek.

"There's Grandpa Norton! He wasn't really my grandfather, but how he used to kick my butt, every time I screwed up around here." Dag smiled in fond remembrance. "The modern schools would take a dim view of this sort of education," he thought, "but Grandpa sure made a man out of me, not to mention the hunting skills he taught me."

"There's his son, R.W.! He hunted here until he was ninety-five years old. He used to sit in the corner of the camp and bitch all of the time, but he had a good heart and nobody ever took him seriously. He always told everybody else how to play poker, but he never invested a penny of his own money.

"And Tom! Probably the funniest man I ever met. Old Tom probably could have made a lot of money doing shows, but he spent his lifetime as an electrician instead, and thinking up crazy things to do around camp.

"John! I don't know whether he came to camp to hunt or to cook. He was an expert at both, and we always enjoyed delicious meals.

"There's my dad! And my son! Dad always protected Dave, but Dave got into the spirit of things and got into trouble anyway. It was all in good fun.

"Dave shot his first buck right over there by Stanley's Peak. God, we were all so proud. We were one big family, and it was like he was everybody's son. What a great experience it was for the boy.

"My brother. Dead now. Man, there was a guy who could shoot.

"Poley, Ramsey, Fat Frank…so many good times.

"We used to sit by that fireplace, late at night, and solve the problems of the world. It's amazing the wisdom that was shared at those times, aside from the foolishness we dreamed up as well.

"In the summer we brought our families here, for a week at a time, to go fishing, or berrying, or just to sit around and relax. I miss those times. Some of the guys have grandchildren now, but they will never have what we had to enjoy."

Alden L. Dumas

Anger and remorse set in again. "Now the land is used for nothing. Like so many other Adirondack historical artifacts of yesteryear, this great hunting lease is a thing of the past."

There was a very small pond beside the old campsite, and a huge boulder by the far bank.

Dag headed that way, skirting the water as he went. There was one more thing he had to check behind the boulder.

Then he would go down to the plane wreck and see if he could help out.

Chapter 40

A big old yellow birch had fallen by the culvert, and Rose and Pete had been tied, by the same rope, to it. The thugs had been kind enough to wrap each in a poncho, but because of the hoods on the things, and the fact that they were back to back on opposite sides of the log, they could not see each other.

"Are they going to kill us now, or later?"

The question came from Rose's lips, as she tossed her head to clear the dripping poncho hood from her face.

They were very uncomfortable, but she was thankful that MacIlwaine had insisted that they be kept dry. Even psychopaths can have their tender side.

Pete struggled at the rope once more. He was desperately trying to get free; damned if he was going to be shot as he was held helplessly like this!

"Stop it, Pete," she demanded, "you're only making the ropes tighter."

"I'm amazed that some of us aren't dead already," he seethed. "That poor Mike is useless to them. Certainly they will kill him soon."

"I think Vitilli senses that, as long as Angela and Doc can care for him, it will keep things a little more peaceful around here," Rose theorized.

"When morning comes, he intends to kill all us men," Pete said calmly, "I think you and the young lady are due for a long dangerous trip."

She nodded, as if he could see her. She didn't want to think about it.

"Your lie about the other party has them scared," she observed. "He's posted guards on all corners. Nobody can enter the camp without being discovered."

"I guess that spells doom for old Dag," he said sadly, "I hate to admit it, but he seems to be our only hope."

"Speaking of hope," Rose said, somewhat brightly, "Let's not sell him short just yet. He's kind of unpredictable. And nobody but us knows he's around."

Meanwhile, up under the tarp, Doc was caring for Mike. "I wish I dared to roll you over," he said, "and see what your back looks like."

"Why don't you make a run for it, Doc?" Mike asked, changing the subject. "They only tie you when you are not working on me. You could probably get out there in the swamp somewhere. I don't think any of these yahoos would dare venture out there."

Doc reached into his medical bag and pulled out a syringe, then a small vial of clear fluid. "This stuff's a muscle relaxant," he said. "I suspect that many of your muscles are very tight, kind of in protest about the way they have been treated. This should ease the pain and make you more comfortable."

"But Doc," Mike went on, "You're our only hope. You could find the other rescue party…"

Doc knew the other rescue party did not exist. He thought that an attempt to escape, and the resulting gunfire, would trigger off a very unfortunate blood bath. As far as he could see, an impulsive act would result in the deaths of the hostages all the sooner.

There were also the visions. The lad he had deserted in that African village so long ago was before him again, and the remorsefulness enveloped him tightly once more. Doc Ginsberg had lost his instincts for survival. To die would be pretty much a welcome escape from the persistent dread he had felt for years.

"My duty is with you," he told Mike, "I will not leave you!"

"What kind of man is this," Mike thought, as the drug kicked in, "who would die for such a hopeless cause?"

"How is he, Doc?" It was Angela's voice.

"Hard to tell," the medic replied. "I tried to reach under him a little and grope about, and I couldn't feel any serious displacement. I just don't dare to roll him around. If there was some kind of emergency, we could fashion some kind of a crude backboard, but I'm going to hold off on that."

Mike laughed through his grogginess. "You should have been here when she dropped the plane," he said, "with me in it!"

Angela's heart sank. "Why did he bring that up again?" she thought. Desperately she needed a kind word from Doc, some kind of assurance that she had not done him any more damage. She knelt by the injured man and buried her head against his chest. Tears flowed once more. Mike sensed that his attempt at a joke had hurt her. The drug must have inhibited his judgment.

He reached for her. She could feel his hand running through her hair.

At that moment, Farley passed by.

"Ain't that cute?" he said in a mocking tone, "Yep, you might as well kiss that boy good-bye."

"You aren't that funny!" Doc scolded.

Farley mocked concern, "Lighten' up! You ain't long for this world either."

Then he walked away.

Trees crashed in the distance, as the ice continued to form, causing cautious eyes to stare off into the mist, suspiciously. The gang of thugs worried collectively, there was no telling when the other rescue party would arrive.

Using some tree branches, Woody had devised a broom- like club he could use to knock the ice from the tarp, to keep it from collapsing. He walked about punching the ceiling above.

Out in the cold rain, Rose looked longingly toward the culvert. "I wonder what Dag is doing?" she asked. The question posed was more to break the boredom, than for any other reason.

"If he's smart," Pete answered bluntly, "he's headed out. His work is done here, and he can't help us."

Chapter 41

Pure luck.

When Dag could see the culvert, a veil of mist blocked any views of the plane. He looked at the rock pile around the structure, and reminisced about the day they had piled them there, to keep it from washing out for the third time.

"It's held well," he whispered to himself.

From upstream, the smell of the smoke titillated his nostrils. "It would be nice to sit and relax by a camp fire," he thought.

"Well," he sighed, "one thing I can do is bring some fire wood with me as I enter camp. I'm not a medic, and this is one job where I can help out."

So he crossed the culvert, and went into the woods below the plane site. He headed up the remnants of an old hunting road he knew. The footing was pretty good, and this particular area was higher than the swamp. It was good hardwood country. Sticks from here would make a much better fire.

Right then a chain saw fired up. Curiously, he slid over in its direction. He had no doubt that the machine was from the plane. "I wonder who is running that thing? Maybe they can use a hand," he thought.

High ground within the Couchsacrage is often cut by small ravines, called guts by woodsmen and hunters, the result of erosion caused by some long lost glacial streams. The activity Dag was investigating was taking place at the bottom of one of these.

Two men were working at wood collection, and after a couple of cuts, the saw was shut off, and before Dag could walk up on them, they began a conversation. By chance he was standing behind a spruce grove, and he would have been hard to see, even if the rainy mist discontinued.

"We sure have pretty hostages," the tall one grinned, and I haven't had me a woman for a long time."

"Pauly," the other man warned, "Vitilli will see them as a bargaining item. Nothing more. You better not damage any goods."

"Oh, Christ, Woody," Pauly replied, annoyed, "You are such a goody-goody. You know that none of them will be alive by tomorrow night. Not likely."

"Well," Woody huffed. "He can't hold a dead person for ransom."

"Vitilli will keep them alive until he gets what he wants, but odds are he'll let Abdul loose on 'em before we're through. It'll be quieter." Pauly predicted.

"God forbid!" Woody answered, as he gathered up the wood. He hoped that he would be far away if Pauly's prophesy came true.

Dag had heard enough. Hostages? Killing people? Who was this Abdul? Who were these guys? Instinctively he sensed that wandering into the camp was the last thing he should do.

Above the culvert there was a rock ledge. It was long and angular, a spur of Baldy Peak Hill, near where the plane should be. Dag decided to climb up there, and sneak over to where he could take a better look.

With the steady rain, and the general noise of the storm, and the incessant mist, it was easy to move about, undetected. Soon he could see the plane, and the tarp, both of which blocked a considerable amount of his view. To get a grip on the situation, he would need to creep a good deal closer.

He could see the brook bed quite well, and the lower edges of Polecat Swamp.

What he saw there disturbed him a great deal: the light green ponchos, with people obviously inside, tied to that broken tree down there. They could hardly move!

There was that Pauly again. He's moving toward the figures. I wonder what he's up to?

Down by the brook, Pauly was feeling mighty good. He had just taken a hit of his substance of choice, and he wanted to have a little fun.

"You're cute," he said to Rose, showing off his brown teeth. Then he looked about suspiciously, "But I'm afraid you could be in some danger. Perhaps a personal favor from you would lead me to do you a favor in return?"

The inference was obvious, and not deserving of an answer.

Pete decided to question the disgusting little man's place in the pecking order instead.

"What could you do?" he needled, "You're not in charge here. Of course, if you had some nerve, and wanted to save your own skin, you could set us free. The law would look upon that act with some favor."

"He wouldn't dare go against Bo or Mac," Rose added, catching on to what Pete was thinking.

The heckling had an effect.

"Shut up!" Pauly ordered, emphatically, looking over his shoulder to see if anyone else was listening. Suddenly he was agitated, and turned to walk away. "You'll be dead, soon enough," he cackled haughtily, then he added with a sickening sweetness, "but I'd sure like to see the goodies underneath that police uniform."

Then he cackled again, and walked back toward the fire.

In spite of herself, Rose pulled at the ropes.

"Cut it out," Pete warned. "What did you tell me a while ago?"

"I want to be free and get my hands on that smart ass!" Rose fumed.

"Him and a few others," Pete agreed.

The night was falling, and the grayish sky got darker and darker. As the hours went by, the campfire seemed to glow all the brighter.

Angela and Doc had been ordered to climb into their sleeping bags, and a rope tied around each of them, to make any escape quite impossible.

The five thugs who were not watching captives, were enjoying a meal, and already the bourbon was flowing.

Meanwhile the captives wondered if they would be fed or not, or if it really made any difference at all.

"You bastards better get a good nights sleep," Vitilli warned his men. "We're getting to hell out of this swamp tomorrow, come hell or high water. Anybody who can't keep up will be left behind."

"Any ideas?" MacIlwaine wanted to know.

"Oh, yes," was the reply. "I've been studying the new official ranger map. I think I know the way."

Vitilli was not one to share. Suspiciously he felt that, if any of the others knew where to go, there might be a deserter or two. He wanted everybody to depend on him.

"Abdul, Farley," Vitilli ordered, "it's your turn to guard those people by the stump. Woody and Martinson can come up here and get something to eat."

For hours, the tight rope had been cutting the circulation to Rose's right arm. Strangely, it was not as annoying now. Perhaps the arm was losing its feeling. Gently she tried to adjust it.

Even though they were tied behind her, her arms moved! They were loose!

"Pete, Pete!" she whispered.

"Yeah, I've noticed," he answered. "But we can't leave now, with fresh guards arriving. We'll have to wait until they are distracted somehow."

"Where will we go?"

"Back up the hill. What Dag called Stanley's Peak, or something. It's dark, and we don't have lights. We can't rush off into the swamp and lose each other. We can feel the gravel of the old road with our feet."

"You're right," Rose added. "We need to find Dag. He has that pistol!"

"Well, he can't be too far," Pete added. "I'll bet I can guess who cut these ropes. Now shut up and act like we're still tied."

Rose could feel the adrenaline rush. There was hope again!

Chapter 42

There is no more terrifying sound in the Adirondack wilderness, than the cry of the lynx. This member of the cat family often hunts the wilds of the Couchsacrage. It is an imposing figure, three or four feet long, with a short bob tail and pointed tufted ears.

It is a secretive creature, spending most of its days in hiding. It is a rare occasion for even the most seasoned woodsman to come across one.

Sometimes, in the darkness, usually after a prey is killed, this animal will let out a cry. This cry is in the form of a high, desperate shriek, not unlike the sound a terrified woman might make, as she is attacked by the blade of a psychopathic slasher, and is brutally murdered by inches, while her desperate screaming intonations cut through the dark wilderness.

Anyone hearing this sound will stop in their tracks, immersed by the frantic reverberations that penetrate the soul.

Many spend a lifetime in the forest, and never hear this call, but those who felt themselves petrified by it once, will never forget it. Campers and hunters will be able to recall exactly where and when they heard it for the rest of their days.

It is a sound that no one ever gets used to. Even hearing it at a later date sends the same chills, initiates the same fears, causing the skin of the listener to crawl once more.

"What to hell is that?" Farley cried.

"I dunno!" was all that Martinson could muster as he felt the hair on the back of his neck begin to rise.

Even Abdul was disturbed. With frightened eyes he glanced back and forth into the primeval darkness.

Vitilli's men were, almost to a man, essentially urban street bullies. They were tough by numbers, to be sure, but the mysteries of the Couchsacrage brought a whole new set of rules.

The cry they heard seemed to come from the bowels of the swamp itself. They stopped all activity, and stood frozen in place by the appalling throes they heard.

From the deep swamp the mists drifted by firelight, like the veils of ghosts. Flashlights could not penetrate through the curtains, either, as the sleet continued to tip tap monotonously away.

Then there was that desperate screech again, closer now, and all eyes searched the darkness for its source as gelid fingers tickled down through their collective spines.

Vitilli, as tough as he was, was not exempt from the terror. He, like the others, felt the panic.

"BAM!"

A gun went off, and everybody jumped and everybody screamed. This was getting to be too much.

"They're free!" MacIlwaine yelled. "They headed up the hill. I had to pull my pistol and rush my shot! I don't think I hit anybody."

Chapter 43

Rose and Pete had not gone far. They were not completely free, not by a long shot. Ropes that held their wrists behind them still held fast. In the pitch blackness they stood back to back and groped at each other to try and loosen them.

"Damn!" Pete hissed, in desperation.

"Well, take it easy!" It was Dag's voice, coming from somewhere in the darkness. "I'll get them."

Soon they were free, and they moved up the hill carefully. There were enough bushes and small trees in the road to make climbing in the darkness very difficult.

"You got your light, Dag?" Rose asked, starting a brief conversation between the two.

"Nope."

"Well, where's your pack?"

"Where we're going."

"Is it safe there?"

"Safer than here."

As they climbed Dag kept saying "here" and "this way" and "watch your step." In the blackness his voice was usually all they had to go on, although he intermittently fired up his cigarette lighter, the only source of illumination he was carrying.

When they reached the top of the hill, Dag led them beyond the turn, and as if guided by some sort of Braille on his feet, verbally led them off the road to the left.

"Stop here," he ordered.

He was gone just a few minutes, and then a light appeared, a beacon to where he was standing.

"Watch your step," he warned. "This door way is mighty low. I'm not going to keep this light on very long. Somebody may be on our trail. But I'll get you inside."

There seemed to be a small, rustic hut there. The inside was cramped, musty, chilly.

"Never thought I'd lead a conservation officer to my outlaw camp," Dag muttered. As soon as everyone had a seat on the dirt floor, he turned out the light.

"If you must know," he went on in the blackness, "when I was still young enough, my boy and I came up here and built this thing, so we could visit here when the mood suited us. It's a long way to carry a pack, but we had a few good times here.

"We built it with some pieces of the old camp that we could salvage. If the light was on you'd notice a couple of crude bunks and one of the old stoves. Believe it or not, some of our dry firewood is still back there, but I'll bet the squirrels or something have the stove pipe blocked, if it hasn't rusted away, that is."

"This structure is against the law," Pete put in.

"Really?" Dag answered. "Don't you ever give up?"

"Let's concentrate on what to do next," Rose interrupted.

"You mean after he's written me a summons?" Dag interjected sarcastically.

Pete ignored him. His voice was calm, but sincere. "I think Miss Bartholemew is safe enough for now," he said. "Come morning Vitilli will try to buy his way out of here, using her as a shield. The other two are probably going to be dead."

"Not Doc?" Dag gasped.

Rose gently grabbed his arm. "We have to focus on what we can do, and not on what we can't help," she said gently.

"You wouldn't have a cell phone with you in your pack?" she added. Obviously she was talking to Dag.

"When I take to the woods, I usually want to be left alone. If I was coming in by myself, I would have brought one, just for an emergency, but I thought you folks had all of that covered."

He sounded sort of embarrassed.

"We need a plan," Pete said hopefully. He had actually accepted Dag's line of reasoning.

Dag still was concerned about his friend. "Let's try and get Doc out of there, too," he suggested.

"Doc is dedicated to Mike," Rose said sadly, "and won't leave his side."

"I know why he won't," Dag added. "The ghosts from his past are going to make him commit suicide."

Then it was silent while they all thought. The brainstorming was tough, and it seemed like they were going nowhere.

Maybe they needed to change the subject for a moment. "There were no cats out there were they, Dag?" Pete asked in a friendlier tone.

"Is it against the law to impersonate a lynx in the swamp?"

Rose laughed. "Enough already!" she exclaimed.

Dag's tone changed, "Well, I do a pretty good coyote too, and I can do a buck snort, but that wouldn't have scared anybody."

"What about a bear?" Rose asked.

"In the deep woods, a bear will hoot," Dag answered. "Of course those idiots would've thought it was an owl. I wasn't going to get in close enough to impersonate a mad mother bear."

"You cut the ropes!" she exclaimed.

"And I was damned quiet when I did that."

"You didn't speak to us?" Rose again.

"I could only get to the far side of the tree, and while I was at it I had to wear a little dead spruce for cover. I couldn't get within whispering distance."

Then they could hear Dag chuckle in the darkness. "I suppose they thought that the little spruce was just some kind of tumbleweed that came and went."

"I doubt that they noticed it," Rose remarked.

"Your gun, Dag! You have a gun!" Pete interrupted.

"My little antique against all of that firepower? You've got to be kidding. Besides, it's not very accurate, and the bullet isn't very big."

"Let's try to think of a way we can use it to rescue Miss Bartholemew. Let's focus on it," Rose suggested.

Dag sighed. "I'll get it. I hope it doesn't get lost. I wanted to give it to Dave someday. Our family has owned this little pistol for generations."

"I wish we could get to a radio or a phone and call for help," Pete went on.

"They're all destroyed, except for the one Vitilli keeps in his pack," Rose said, "and that was just for us to call in bogus reports. He'll destroy it before we get to use it."

"And he wants all of us dead," Pete added. "It will be extremely risky if any of us are even seen."

"He doesn't even know about me," Dag said.

"We've thought of that," Rose added, "Maybe that can help us somehow."

"Shhhh! What's that?" Pete whispered urgently.

It was Vitilli's voice, about fifty yards away.

"Hey ranger, copper! Come out now or we'll kill a hostage. I swear to God we will."

He had been calling this message, over and over, as he, MacIlwaine, and Woody had climbed the hill. He hoped someone was there to hear it.

Chapter 44

NEWS RELEASE (TV):

"Bernard Gordon with a WGHZ bulletin:

"The ice storm enveloping northern New York State continues. Road crews have been very diligent in their task of cleaning the slippery and clogged highways in the storm area.

"Power lines in the ice storm area are still a mess, and only those who own private generators have electricity.

"Recent news is not all good. Near the small Adirondack hamlet of Eagle's Aerie, a small store that dealt in camping and fishing supplies has been ransacked, and the owners murdered. No money was stolen. Police at this point are baffled at the motives behind the crime, but as soon as they can report to the area in force, they will be working to solve it.

"In a matter that may be related, two young police officers, identified as Donald Jones and Luke Williams, have not been in contact with command post for over twenty four hours. Nor has their squad car been seen.

"If anyone has any information regarding either of the aforementioned items, please call your local police station.

"And now for more happy news!

"Word from the depths of the Adirondack wilderness indicates that the rescue team that has gone in to find the daughter of Governor Harry Bartholemew has met with great success.

"Rescue team leader, Forest Ranger Peter Randolph, reports by cell phone that Pilot Ron Marks, Angela Bartholemew, and her escort, Michael Howell, are all in excellent mental and physical condition.

"No further rescue efforts will be necessary until the weather clears.

"According to Ranger Randolph, they will sit by the camp fire and 'chill out' until the rescue helicopter arrives.

"According to station WGHZ's meteorologist, June Barlow, there will be at least one more day of this relentless storm over the northeast, before any chance of clearing will be possible.

"We are so happy to report this great news about the governor's daughter and her companions!

"Soon they will be all home, and safe!

"They are probably sitting around a camp fire right now, singing and telling scary stories.

"More later. Please stay tuned."

Chapter 45

"Time's almost up," Vitilli snarled loudly. "I'll be killing me some hostages soon."

He had climbed the road from the culvert to the fork, and he and two of his comrades stood there, waving their flashlights about.

"One last time…" he began anew.

"I'm here!" It was Rose's voice in the darkness. "Turn out your lights!"

"Where are you?" Vitilli asked.

"I'm hidden. I won't come out. If you don't douse those lights, I'm gone."

"Shut the lights," was Vitilli's order. When it was totally black again, he asked, "Where's the ranger?"

"I can't find him," Rose lied. "Maybe I can tomorrow when it is light."

In truth, Pete and Dag stood nearby. Dag held his little pistol in hand, in case anybody made a grab for Rose.

"I want you and the ranger to turn yourselves in," Vitilli went on, "otherwise we'll begin to kill the hostages one by one."

"This is not a threat," Rose negotiated, "You will kill them anyway. You just want to add me and my partner to your list. What's in it for us?"

The cold rain continued. They could feel the icy pellets in the darkness.

One of Vitilli's men made a move to come closer. Rose could hear the rustling of his rain gear.

"Tell your men to stand still," Rose warned, "or I'm gone, and this conversation is over."

In the darkness, Dag held his pistol ready, although no one could see anything at all.

"Mac, Woody! Stand still, dammit!" Vitilli barked. Then in a sweeter voice, he said, "There is another option. If you can guarantee us safe passage out of here, we don't have to kill anybody."

"That's better," Rose answered. "How can I help you?"

"Let's say," Vitilli proposed, "that you and the little lady accompany us out of here. We'll tie the others. They'll be okay until the storm clears. Nobody dies, and we all go home."

"Why do you need hostages anyway?" What have you done?" Rose wanted to know.

"Drop it lady. You could know too much," Vitilli warned. "Then the bargaining chips would be a lot different."

There was a silence for a while, as Rose thought about the offer. Finally she said, "When I find my partner, we'll talk it over. We'll get back to you."

"Get back to us? How the hell can you do that?"

"You have lanterns in camp. Send a man back up here and have him set one on the road. After my partner shows up, and if we can think of a compromise, we'll go down to the culvert and set it there. You can come over and talk to us, alone."

"What if I just start killing hostages?" Vitilli threatened again, as if of a one-track mind.

"Kill them. Go ahead! And we'll see you in court. It'll be a spectacular trial. But remember, the ranger and I could walk out of here tonight. The only way we'll stay is if those people are alive and well."

Rose's voice was steady and convincing.

Vitilli was quietly enraged. This cop and her buddy, the ranger, had to be eliminated. All of this was very clear now. There were only two of them, and he had their packs and they had no weapons. Time would tell who was in the driver's seat.

"Okay," he said, finally, "Let's go back to camp boys." Then, to make sure he got in the last word, he warned, "Just remember, I'm not a patient man."

Chapter 46

For something to do, Martinson, Farley, and Pauly had fashioned a lean-to of their own, out of a few seedlings and two tents. They had found a level spot a little farther upstream, and to make things cozier, had built a campfire of their own as well.

They presently sat around it, and passed a bottle of bourbon around, and smoked cigarettes and laughed and joked and talked about whatever young punks talk about as they sit around a campfire.

Abdul had made his own quarters on the opposite side of the brook, under some boulders whose arrangement made a natural cover. He seemed not to need a fire, though the glow from the other two fires reflected off his shelter just the same. The others could see his shining beady eyes staring back at them from the darkness of his little hole.

Doc, Angela, and Mike were now tied securely inside their sleeping bags. They were under the protection of the tarp, but their fire was dwindling due to lack of fuel.

"I hope Woody comes back soon, "Doc said quietly. Woody was the only member of the gang who had placed his bag under the tarp, and he seemed to be making it his project to keep the fire going.

"I hope they don't catch our friends," Angela said. "Personally, I think they should go for help."

"By the time help got here, they wouldn't be of much use to us," Mike reflected.

"I guess that's true." Angela agreed, softly. "I don't want to die, but if it's going to happen, I don't want my killers to get away with it."

"You have a chance," Mike responded hopefully, "Maybe, if they use you for a hostage, you will be spared."

"What about you, Mike? What will happen to you?" she asked nervously.

"They aren't going to be bothered with a cripple," he concluded realistically, "especially a cripple who is a witness."

"Why do these people want to do us harm?" Angela sobbed.

It was Doc's turn to speak. "Obviously, they are on the lam from someplace else. Anyone who can place their presence here at this time would be a very dangerous witness."

"Then we're all dead?" There was numbness to Angela's voice.

"I'm afraid it doesn't look good at this point," Doc said flatly, "Unless our friends can think of something. There has to be some hope."

213

Angela turned her head in the direction of her consort.

"Mike," she cried, "I want you to know that I think I've fallen in love with you. I want you to know that now, before something happens."

Mike looked at her tenderly, but did not respond right away. He was trying to sort it all out, and he concluded that it be best if Angela was not overly infatuated with him at this time. It was looking like he was going to die tomorrow, and he wanted to buffer her emotions when it happened.

It was this context that forced him to say, "In the real world, wouldn't you want a man who isn't paralyzed from the waist down?"

"Please give me more credit than that," she pleaded. "I wish I could hold you now. You would see that I mean what I say."

Tears began to drip down Mike's cheeks as well. Silently he cursed the events that had led to the situation they were in. The girl of his dreams was falling in love with him and at the same time it looked like they would both die soon.

To change the mood of remorsefulness that he felt, he turned to Doc. "The next time they untie you, Doc, "he suggested, "Run like hell!"

The haunting memories from the past returned to the medic, and he said once again, "I promised you that I won't leave, and I won't. If they kill you, they will have to kill me too."

Doc closed his eyes and tried to rest, but the screams of the tortured from that African village of long ago, seemed to rip across his eardrums once again.

"Maybe all of this will be over at last," he whispered to himself.

Chapter 47

The lantern had sat, glowing, at the fork in the road for several minutes. It had been decided, after a long deliberation, that Pete should retrieve it, while covered by Rose, who held Dag's pistol in the darkness.

Any thug who would try to interfere would be shot. That had been agreed to. Vitilli had to be shown that underhanded breaches in faith would not be tolerated.

Such an act would lead to a brutal repercussion, that was a fact, but the rescue group had decided that the likelihood of saving Doc or Mike was practically nil anyhow. They had to take some chances somewhere. Angela had become their main focal point.

So Pete moved rapidly out into the open, and just as quickly snuffed out the light.

In the total darkness they could move to the relative safety of Dag's little cabin.

"Wait!"

A voice in the darkness.

It was pitch black again. Very little to fear.

"Please!"

The voice once more. Rose thought she recognized it.

"Is that you Woody?" she asked. "Be careful, we do have a weapon here!"

"I want to talk. I want you to trust me," Woody answered.

"How do we know that?" Rose asked.

"In a moment, go back to where the lantern was," Woody replied, "you will find a token of my sincerity."

"I'll set the lantern back where it was." It was Pete's voice. "When you turn it on, stay where we can see you."

"Yes sir! Glad you are found!"

After awhile the light was glowing again. They could see Woody's outline beside it.

Cautiously, Pete moved in beside him, and looked on the ground.

"Well, I'll be damned!" he exclaimed. "My pistol!"

"Yes sir! Holster and all!" Woody replied. "Now can we talk?"

There was a pause while Pete strapped the weapon to his waist once more.

"Who are these guys?" Rose wanted to know.

"Killers! Drug dealers! Mobsters! You name it!" Woody proclaimed.

"Why are you with them?" Pete asked sternly.

"I don't know. I wanted things. I wanted easy money. One thing led to another. Now I'm sucked in. It's all gone too far. I want to get out."

"Why didn't you run?" Pete again.

"Don't you know how Vitilli is about witnesses? He's the same way regarding loyalty. If he knew what was going on right now, I'd be a dead man."

"How come you are here, in this storm, in the middle of the Couchsacrage, of all places?" Rose inquired.

"Oh, God! Some cops got killed. We had to make a run for it. Other people got killed. I had no place to go, I had to go along. I'm not like them…Oh, man, I screwed up my life and I let my family down!" There was a catch to Woody's voice, as if he was going to cry.

"I can face jail for doing the drug deliveries," he went on, "I deserve that. But I won't be a party to all this killing. I haven't killed anybody, and I don't want to. I want to be on your side."

"Thank you for coming forward," Rose said kindly, "I hope you are sincere. But I can't promise you anything…"

"I know," Woody said. "But I'm with you, they can't tie me to any killings. I've already witnessed enough, and it all makes me sick."

Then he added, with desperation in his voice, "Oh, how did I get tangled up in a mess like this?"

"Are you willing to help us?" Rose asked.

"Can I earn freedom?" Would you let me go? Even if I testify in court, they will hunt me down and kill me," Woody pleaded.

Rose sighed. "I'll have to arrest you when this is over. But there is hope that you can do your time and start over." Then she added in a hopeful tone, "It is your only chance!"

"I guess you're right," Woody sighed. "But I never killed anybody," he repeated.

"Yeah, right!" Pete admonished, "Like the drugs you deliver don't kill people!"

"Take it easy, Pete," Dag said softly.

To Woody this was another voice in the darkness, a strange unknown voice.

"Give the kid a break," it went on, "Maybe we can put him to use."

"Yes," Woody agreed. "If I help, you can testify on my behalf. But what can I do?" Hearing a previously unknown voice had shocked him.

"I have a plan," the man with the new voice put in, "We can go down to the plane site, and surround the place. There are only three logical exits. Woody can return to camp, and tonight, when everybody is asleep, he can untie Angela and lead her out of there. No matter which way he goes, one of us can lead him to safety."

"I have my gun back!" Pete interrupted, as if it would help.

"Well, whoopy doo!" Dag exclaimed. "They have at least five, and high powered at that. Who are you, Doc Holliday? This isn't the O.K. Corral."

"We'll need you to cover us while the escape is on," Rose told Pete. "With Angela, we can all make a break back down the railroad bed tonight. There would be no point in waiting until morning."

"Mike and Doc are goners, I guess," Dag sighed. "We can't help them."

It was quiet again, as they each reflected upon what was before them.

"I'll do the best I can," Woody finally said. "Before I go back to camp, there are a few things I'd like to leave with you."

He reached under his coat, an act that forced Rose to instinctively lift up Dag's small weapon again. But Woody produced a package.

"More food," he said. "I thought you could use it."

Then he reached behind him, and pulled something off his back.

"My pride and joy," he announced. "My old hunting rifle. They don't make them like this any more. Could you keep it safe for me? It'll be too cumbersome if I have to run with Angela through the swamp."

"I'd be glad to," Rose replied.

"Then, it's time to go," Woody sighed, reluctantly.

"Wait!" Dag cried, as if motivated by some sudden impulse. "Rose, can I have my gun?"

In the dim lantern light, Woody could see the police officer handing the stranger something. Then the man walked over to him.

"And this is my pride and joy," Dag said stiffly, "and I don't want to lose it either."

He handed the weapon to the young outlaw.

"Now, it's loaded," Dag continued, "so be careful. I want you to smuggle this to Doc. Understand? If they kill him, I hope he takes somebody with him."

In a moment, Woody was gone.

They turned the lantern off, and shuffled toward the little cabin in the darkness.

Dag sighed. He was sure that he would never see his great grandfather's pistol again.

Chapter 48

"This will be our rendezvous spot," Pete announced, "If anything goes wrong, come here. Somebody will meet you here."

"I'm glad my little outlaw cabin is of some use to you," Dag said, a pleased smile on his lips.

"Well, the conservation law says it shouldn't be here," Pete reminded him.

"It's a law that sort of points out the one little flaw in the democratic system." Dag philosophized.

"What's that?" Pete asked haughtily.

"A misinformed majority can inflict a lot of pain and misery on an innocent minority."

Pete tried to ignore the observation.

They were putting what they had for gear in order. Soon they would have to head down the hill and into the swamp. Everything had to be as ready as possible.

The problem was that the only supplies they had was what Dag had brought in his pack. It was a skimpy selection.

"One flash light. Dag, you take that," Pete insisted, you have the farthest to go."

"You're right," Dag agreed. "I really can't go where I need to be without it."

"And besides," Rose joked, "Pete and I have been up and down that hill in the pitch blackness so many times that we could do it blindfolded."

Her little comment made them all chuckle.

"We'll leave the lantern here, "Pete said. "That way we can find it if we need it."

"Woody's gun?" Dag asked.

"Too unwieldy," Rose commented. "Besides, I promised to keep it safe. I could trip and break something."

"Let me see it for a second," Dag requested.

Carefully he removed the weapon from its sheath.

"Oh, it's a beauty! Savage 300, lever action. I used one as a boy. Dave, my son, has it now. A wide-view scope too! How I'd love to shoot it! It brings back so many memories."

Dag busied himself putting it back away again. "No wonder Woody is so protective of it," he added.

"We all have compasses?" Pete asked.

The others answered in the affirmative.

"Then we're ready to go," Pete said. "No telling when Woody can make a break for it."

As they got up to leave, Rose asked Dag, "When you and Dave came up here to this little hideaway, how did you spend your time?"

"We fished mostly, and hiked around. The brook is loaded with little brook trout, "Dag answered.

"The limit is five," Pete reminded him. Dag could not see the amused smirk on the ranger's face.

"Of course," Dag replied, feigning serious, "In ten minutes we were done fishing for the day. The rest we left in the brook, to save for the next party who was bound to show up back here at any minute."

It was almost like they were beginning to understand each other. All three laughed as they headed for the swamp.

It was the last moment of levity the three of them would ever enjoy together.

Chapter 49

Doc couldn't believe what he had found.

He had reached in his bag for some pills to relieve his heartburn, and there it was…Dag's pistol!

He recognized it right away, the antique that his friend cherished so passionately. How did it get to where he had found it?

The thugs that guarded them, especially Pauly, were constantly eying Doc's medical bag. Doc could feel that Pauly continuously longed for a new kind of cheap thrill, and the young punk no doubt felt that there was something in the bag that would provide it. It was only a matter of time before Doc's medical supplies would be public property.

Keeping the gun in the bag was a bad idea. But where could he hide it, yet still keep it accessible?

Finally, he slid over to his patient. "Open your hand, Mike?" he said, and he slipped the weapon into Mike's fingers. "Keep this handy, and hidden," was the command.

Mike chuckled. "Like a pea shooter against mortar fire," he laughed. "Where did you get this thing?"

"Damned if I know," Doc whispered, "but it gives us a little hope."

Mike tucked it in his belt, and tried to visualize a circumstance where it could save them all. No probable scenario came to mind.

"At least let it help save Angela," he prayed.

Angela was sitting nearby. She had brought a pot of hot water, and began to clean up the supper dishes. It was something to keep herself occupied, even though the activity by now seemed pointless.

Woody came by with an armful of wood, and began stacking it carefully by the fireplace.

He was close enough for all three to hear his conversation.

"Be ready," he said to Angela, "I'm to take you out of here, to the police woman. Tonight."

To Angela this was simply another head game. Here she was, surrounded by some of the real lowlives of society, and they all had to take turns harassing her. Now it was Woody's turn.

Still, she thought, Woody had been a perfect gentleman up to now. This brought a little credence to his statement.

"Listen to him," Doc ordered. The sudden appearance of Dag's pistol now had an explanation. "He's probably telling you the truth."

Mike was also paying close attention.

"The forest ranger and the police woman, and some stranger I never met before," Woody whispered enthusiastically, "will be waiting in the woods for us. When the others go to sleep, I will come and get you."

The mention of the "stranger" was all the proof Doc needed. The stranger had to be Dag. Now Doc was positive about Woody's credibility.

"Woody's telling the truth!" Doc insisted, again.

"Where do we go?" Angela asked, still not sure what she wanted to do.

"Anyplace. They said they would find us," Woody answered.

"We'll get shot!" she worried.

"It will be dangerous," Woody agreed, "but nobody wants you to stay here and face the inevitable."

"That's for sure!" Mike agreed. He would use the new pistol for a distraction if he had to. "Please, honey," he pleaded, "You have to go. This will be your only chance."

Angela looked desperately at the man she loved.

Then she turned to Woody again. "What of Mike?" she asked, hoping for the impossible.

"I'm sorry," Woody answered.

"They probably have a plan for us later," Doc put in, forcing a hopeful tone.

"They will kill Mike, and they will kill you," Angela deducted desperately. "I don't want to leave!"

Mike looked at her angrily now. "You have to trust Woody. It's our only hope!" He nodded in the direction of the young thugs by the fire. "Look at the weapons they have!"

"Besides," Woody lied, "Doc is right. The others will come up with a plan to get Mike and Doc out of here later."

Woody was in too deep already. His existence now seemed to depend on Angela making her escape. He would do or say anything to get her out of this camp site.

"Why are you involved?" she asked suspiciously.

Woody looked back and forth. It was time for another lie.

"I'm an undercover agent," he said. "I've been on this case for quite some time. The turn of events has forced my hand. Things are a little out of control now."

Angela did not sense the falseness. Agents had surrounded her a lot during her lifetime. Perhaps Woody was telling the truth.

Still, she hedged. How could she leave Mike behind?

Mike could sense her apprehension.

"Look at me!" Mike ordered. "Woody has given me a pistol, that I have concealed here in my sleeping bag. Maybe Doc and I can use it later. Two will be easier to save than three. It will help us a great deal if you will go with Woody!"

As the rain continued to pelt the top of the tarp, and the ice continued to form on any solid mass it hit, Angela's moist blue eyes shimmered in the firelight.

"Okay," she sighed softly, "I'll go. But I'll wait for you, as long as it takes."

Chapter 50

The three rescuers could stay together until they reached the culvert at the base of the hill. It was slow going. The use of a flashlight seemed to be too dangerous, as the mists of the Couchsacrage were more translucent than opaque. Any strange glow, seen from the enemy camp, would suddenly arouse suspicion.

So the use of light was limited to brief flashes. The rest of the time they had to negotiate all of the obstacles in the complete darkness.

"Thank God we've been up and down this way before," Rose breathed to herself.

The big question was when Woody would see an opportunity to make a break for it. They would need to be in position for hours, in the freezing rain, waiting.

It was Rose who slid off into the forest first. One possible escape route, would be to ford the brook directly, past where the strange Abdul was holed up, and dash into the forest there.

This would be a chilly choice, with an immediate danger of hypothermia. Should this take place, Rose intended to escort them up the hill immediately to Dag's camp, and rusty stove pipe or not, attempt to build a fire in the old stove, and hope for the best.

She resolved that, after the escape was complete, and even if the fugitives did not come to her, she would return immediately to the little cabin and try to get the stove in working order, in case it was needed.

Between the brook and where she had to stand, there was an embankment. She nestled in among some spruces there. The branches were cold to the touch, but, by crouching down low, she had a great deal of protection from the rain.

"Now to wait," she whispered.

Pete would guard the culvert escape route. He had to be careful here, because Vitilli and his men would be watching this area carefully. It also would present a long run for Woody and Angela before they could enter the safety of the swamp and hide. Pete had taken this assignment because he had the pistol, and he would use it if he had to.

He lowered himself below the embankment on the lower end of the culvert. Although the plane site was nearly a hundred yards away, he could see what was going on there pretty well.

There was one other feasible escape route: upstream and into the heart of Polecat Swamp.

It offered the quickest exit from the crash site, but it would be a nightmare to guide the fugitives to safety through there.

Once Angela had escaped, the rescue party anticipated that Vitilli would have searchers up and down the road and at the culvert area. Below the culvert there was some very high water, so bypassing it would be almost impossible. The road itself would be too narrow to be able to sneak by undetected. Anyone in Polecat Swamp would have to exit another way.

Polecat Swamp was like a big piece of pie, the farther upstream one went, the wider it got, and the harder it was to cross back to where the railroad bed ran beside it. This marsh offered all kinds of hazards, from holes and spruce groves and broken trees, to the brook, which aimlessly meandered about, and perhaps was now impossible to cross due to high water and beaver dams.

This was Dag's assignment. Presently he passed by Pete's position, and he now had to get to his post by negotiating the contours on the backside of Baldy Peak Hill. Then he would need to slide down various steep cliff sides to a spot next to the crash site, just beyond the plane wreckage. This was all very time consuming and dangerous in the blackness.

He prayed that Woody and Angela would not head toward him. In the daylight he could possibly cross this morass. In the old days, he probably could have negotiated the swamp in the dark after he had seen what obstacles it had to offer, but on this night it would offer too many challenges.

After being away for many years, he would be asked to guide someone across a variety of unknown perils in the blackness and the ice storm.

"C'mon," he mumbled, as if making a joke. "I'm good, but I'm not that good."

Chapter 51

It was after midnight.

Vitilli, tired of watching for the signal light from Rose, had decided to crawl into his tent and get some sleep.

Five of his men still milled around the camp, and it was apparent that Farley, Martinson, and Pauly were making a party out of it.

"Get to sleep, you stupid bastards!" Vitilli warned. "Tomorrow, bright and early, we're out of here, as fast as we can go."

He greatly feared that the weather would clear, and he would still be in the swamp. The map had shown a route, back toward Bunchberry, that followed the railroad bed almost exclusively. He felt that it could be traveled in a day, if they moved fast enough. He hoped that the weather would provide cover for twenty-four more hours.

"Must be she couldn't find the ranger," he mumbled to MacIlwaine, who was already snoring, again referring to Rose and her awaited signal.

Soon Vitilli was asleep as well.

Woody and Angela sat poised and ready, adrenaline racing through their blood. Across the brook Abdul stared back.

"Doesn't he ever sleep?" Angela muttered. She was repairing a torn sweat shirt, using a sewing kit that had been found on the plane. Nobody cared about the sweat shirt, but it was an excuse for her not to be tied inside of her sleeping bag at this time of night.

Woody stood by her, as if guarding her should she attempt to escape.

The illusion was not hard to pull off, as the others paid them little mind. Except Abdul, whose attention dampened thoughts of an immediate getaway.

Doc and Mike were already tied. Ropes around the outside of their bags made movement, even of their arms, almost impossible.

Another bottle of bourbon was brought out, and opened by the revelers. Woody could see the powder on Pauly's face, indicating that the young punk was enjoying an extra special high.

The three thugs were engaged in an animated conversation, laughing gleefully. Here and there they would look back in Angela's direction. Even from where they sat, Woody could see a wildness in their eyes.

At first, Woody thought this was a positive turn. Whatever shenanigans they were up to would surely distract Abdul, and when that would happen, they could make a run for it.

Certainly, waiting for those three clowns to go to sleep was going to take awhile.

Then things turned very bad indeed.

Farley left the other campfire, and headed toward Woody and Angela. Pauly was close behind, with Martinson watching from their lean to.

Farley positioned himself next to Mike.

Mike was fully awake, anticipating Angela and Woody's flight to safety. He wanted to witness the event, possibly the last thing he would ever enjoy. He expected that he and Doc would be killed soon after.

He was tied fast. The little gun in his belt would be of no use except at very close range.

Why was Farley standing over him, with a wild, evil grin on his face?

Already Pauly was reaching his hand down to Angela.

"We're going to have us a little show," he announced contemptuously. "On your feet, Goldilocks."

He began to pull her back to their lean-to, and away from the tarp where Woody sat. Farley still stood by Mike, who could only lay on the ground.

Soon Pauly was shoving Angela to the ground next to the three thug's camp fire. He staggered in his drunkenness. He grinned foolishly.

"We are now going to have a strip show," he slurred. "Haven't you all wondered what goodies this little darlin' hides beneath all those baggy clothes?"

Martinson clapped. So did Farley, who was still standing over Mike. Abdul and Woody just stared ahead, showing no emotion.

Woody was frozen. He had no weapon, and he couldn't fight the three of them anyway. He would have to keep his composure and look for an opening.

Angela was indignant. "There is no way I would take my clothes off in front of vermin like you!" she spat.

Pauly grinned. He looked blankly at Farley, and shrugged.

With that, Farley kicked Mike in the side, with all of the force he had.

Mike screamed in pain. His breath was gone. He attempted to curl up and he desperately gasped for air, tears forming on his face.

Doc was also awake, and shouted epithets at the attackers.

Farley pulled his pistol. "Shut the hell up," he warned, "shut up."

Doc was quiet. Not for himself, but he hoped that they would not abuse Mike any more.

Woody slid toward where Angela was. There might be a chance to do something. He didn't know what, but he felt he should keep close to her.

From the bushes across the brook, Rose was appalled by what she saw. Of course she could do nothing.

At the culvert an enraged Pete could barely keep still. He could barely fight off the anger he could feel building up. He began to inch forward.

Dag, on the other hand, could barely see the plane site from his post in the swamp. He didn't have much knowledge of what was going on. He hoped he would be able to tell when it was time to go back to his camp.

"Okay, darlin'," Pauly smiled again. "Take it off or your little buddy boy gets another kick."

Tears of rage streamed down Angela's face, and a numbness came over her. Mike was possibly crippled for life and all of this was making matters worse. She sensed that taking her clothes off would only be the beginning of a humiliating and torturous night, but what were her choices?

"Please," she begged, "don't kick him again."

She pulled off her raincoat, and unbuttoned the flannel shirt that once had belonged to the pilot. As she went about her repulsive ordeal she tried to separate her body from her mind. She thought of home and the gardens beyond her house, anything to distract her conscious mind from what she had to do.

The flannel shirt and the sweatshirt were now on the ground, and she stood before them wearing the frilly blouse from her previous world.

"Take it off, take it off," mocked Pauly, as Martinson grinned sickeningly.

Mike was barely coming to. He was in excruciating pain. Nausea overcame him, and while he vomited the stoic Angela was yards away, standing naked from the waist up, bravely clenching her teeth as low-lives hooted and raved.

Woody had already collected the clothes she had already thrown down, and put them in a pile. If they could make a break for it, they would have to go.

"Now the boots, and the rest of it," Farley laughed, from a distance.

"Good God!" Angela shuddered. "Will this ever end?"

Even though she stood half naked in the sleet, her mortification and shock numbed her from the cold. She reached down and began to untie her boot.

"That's enough! Party's over!"

It was Pete's voice, loud and calm.

He moved up the brook from the culvert, holding his pistol at the ready as he came. He waved it toward one thug and then the other.

"Put your gun down, godammit," he said to Farley, and the little weasel-like man did as he was told.

Pete had slipped into camp, and as he moved forward, he tried to control the complete rage that consumed him.

"Get your clothes, Angela," the ranger ordered, "We're leaving!"

Then he turned to the others. "You are all beyond any description I could think of. Words like disgusting and repulsive just don't do it!"

Suddenly, a gun went off, three times, and blood spouted from the ranger's chest.

Angela began to scream, over and over, as Pete fell, head first to the ground. He was already dead.

The shots, Woody knew, came from Abdul's position across the brook.

Everybody turned to look. It was the chance Woody had been waiting for. He grabbed Angela's hand and headed upstream, toward the heart of Polecat Swamp.

Chapter 52

Gunshots!

There was a flurry of activity everywhere.

"There they go!" Martinson screamed. He could see Woody and Angela heading up the brook. They were not yet beyond the glow of the campfires.

All of the noise had awakened Vitilli, who now stood in front of his tent, wearing only his underwear. In a moment he could sense that his prized hostage had fled.

Near to him stood Farley, staring blankly ahead, with his pistol, or what once had been Rose's pistol, at his feet.

"Get after them!" Vitilli screamed. Then he turned toward Martinson, who was frantically searching for his own weapon, one that once had belonged to Police Officer Luke Williams.

"You too!"

Farley and Martinson were still dressed in their regular outdoor attire, so soon they were in pursuit. There was no doubt where the fugitives had gone. To the right was the deep brook, and to the left were the steep ledges of Baldy Peak Hill. Woody and Angela had to be traveling up the narrow strip between.

The sudden gunfire had sent Pauly sprawling for cover. Now he stupidly rose from the ground, covered with mud. He had no weapon to use for a chase, and besides he was hopelessly stoned. He sank to his knees, and put his head in his hands.

Abdul still glared menacingly from his perch across the stream. From there he was in no position to chase anyone.

"Guard the road, Abdul," Vitilli commanded, "you and Mac, in case they double back."

From her vantage point across the brook, Rose was totally stunned by what she had seen. A paralyzing weakness took command of her knees, and for a moment she was unable to move.

But she had been trained to react, and some sort of strategy had to be considered. She fought to calm herself down and to think clearly.

From what she had witnessed, she was quite certain that Pete was dead, and there was no way she, being alone and unarmed, could do anything for Mike and Doc. Angela and Woody were heading upstream, where, she prayed, Dag would intercept them and take care of them.

What could she do? Not much. She headed for the little cabin at the top of the hill, the designated rendezvous point.

She hoped to make the little cabin ready, for whatever emergency might come.

She would load up Woody's rifle as well, and guard the top of the hill.

"You never know," she thought.

Chapter 53

As soon as they were out of the glow of the campfires, Woody stopped long enough to hand Angela some clothes. Quickly she donned the sweatshirt, flannel shirt, and jacket.

"Stow the rest," she gasped in the darkness, and her frilly blouse and her brassiere were tossed aside.

"Let's go," she said, when things were in order. It was just in time, for the flashlights of Farley and Martinson could be seen coming up the brook bed. One was pointed downward, for footing, but the second one sent a scanning beam forward.

"There they are!" screamed the agitated Farley, and he pulled his pistol and let fly with a wild shot.

The rains continued to fall.

Woody was worried. He was forced to turn on his own light. He could see by the obstacles before him that the going would be slow. They would not be able to get out of pistol range, and they certainly couldn't stop.

It was a real dilemma. They couldn't move rapidly in the pitch blackness, but to use a light would illuminate an easy target for their pursuers.

"Bring her back, Woody!" Martinson yelled. "Bo ain't gonna like this!"

This made Woody want to move all the faster. Vitilli would kill him, that was for sure. He shined the flashlight ahead. Obviously, the only path of escape was before them. It was narrow and predictable.

Another wild shot rang through the woods behind them. The nature of the swamp and the unforgiving weather did not allow them to discern where the bullet hit, nevertheless Woody and Angela tried to step up their pace even more.

Where was this guy who was supposed to help them?

"This way!" a shout from the blackness to their left. Suddenly another light was flashing from between two trees, and an arm reached out and grabbed Woody's sleeve.

"I'm Dag," the man announced. "We've met."

There was no time for further conversation. As if led by some kind of instinct, Woody pushed Angela in front of him.

Already Dag had moved on ahead. By waving his light, he could see the cliff side in front of him. Roots hung down to offer handholds and footholds. This was the route he intended to follow.

Up Dag went, temporarily pocketing his light.

There was no time to waste. Angela was right behind him, climbing hand over hand, using any foothold available. It was risky, but Woody tried to flash his light here and there so she could see the next set of roots. It was slow and terrifying. The same dilemma.

Woody's turn. He had to negotiate the same set of problems, with Dag trying to show the way here and there. Up he went.

The mountainside was a series of ledges, none any higher than ten or fifteen feet. As soon as they reached the top of one, it was on to another.

At first, Farley and Martinson, still groggy from their evening with bourbon, missed the turn off. This bought time. But the constant flashing of light, as necessary as it was, attracted the thugs attention once again. Soon they were climbing the lower ledge as Dag's party reached the base of the second.

It was frustrating for the pursued. Moving in the total darkness was nearly impossible, especially up through the steep escarpments. Yet to illuminate their position was almost worse.

Except they had to keep moving, and they couldn't move fast enough if they couldn't see.

The lights had to be on more than they were off, and that was bad, very bad.

Dag had reached the top of the third level, and pulled the struggling Angela up behind him. He was totally winded, and had to rest. Very few men his age would have been able to go on much further.

Farley and Martinson weren't far behind. They were younger, and could go on a lot longer than Dag could. They had weapons and could shoot on a whim. Since the people they pursued were unarmed, they could keep their lights on as much as they wished. The dilemma once more.

Woody had just reached the top of the third level when disaster struck.

From where he was, Dag heard the report of the pistol, and he could see the flash of flame as it released its deadly missile.

It might have been a lucky shot, but a bullet hit Woody in the back, and exited through his chest. Blood splattered everywhere.

"Oh God!" Woody screamed, "I'm hit bad." He dropped his flash light, and it went rolling back down among the rocks.

Angela also screamed, and fought back the hysterics that wanted to consume her. She helped the panting Dag to pull Woody up to the top. Woody was already in convulsions, fighting for air that could not enter his shattered chest.

"Oh God!" he ranted pitifully, in a voice barely audible, "I don't want to die this way. Oh Mother, I have let you down…"

"What will we do?" Angela sobbed, panic in her voice, "We can't just leave him!"

The anxiety made Dag all the more worn out. As poor Woody lay dying next to him, he knew that they couldn't run any more.

"Quiet!" he said, in a stage whisper.

He handed Angela his flashlight. "Take it to the next ledge," he ordered, "and put it up on the bank as high as you can reach. Then get away from it and hide somewhere."

Alden L. Dumas

"What about Woody?" she cried.

"One thing at a time," the old man replied.

Already Farley and Martinson were ascending the ledge. In minutes they would be breaking over the top. It was Dag's hope that they would focus on the light beyond.

Next to them was a sturdy beech tree, with a long branch that had been in the climbers' way as they had broken over top of the ledge.

Carefully and quietly, using all of his strength, Dag pulled this branch back across the flat, table like landing. From her position Angela could see his profile, as he puffed and strained in the rain, trying to get footing on the icy surface.

The limb was heavy, and Dag prayed for the strength to hold it.

Immediately Angela recognized his plan. She moved back down from her position and forward to help him.

When Angela was beside him, and he could feel the relief her strength provided, he said. "When I holler, let go!"

The glimmer of Farley's light soon could be seen reflecting off the mist, and almost immediately the two thugs were standing at the top.

"There they are," Farley cried in his squeaky voice, referring to the light beyond. "Take a shot, Hank!"

"Look!" Martinson replied, as he spotted the body near his feet, "We got Woody!"

"Now!" shouted Dag, and the heavy limb whipped across the ledge top, gaining momentum as it went.

248

It hit Farley in the chest with all of its force, and he screamed as he fell, down the cliff and into the rocks below.

Martinson grabbed the limb, and held on, but everything he had carried, including his light and his pistol, followed the terrified Farley. Martinson dangled precariously.

The limb swayed to and fro in the darkness, and Martinson held on with all the strength he had. He realized that he would have to work his way back to the cliff, and then descend carefully in the darkness. There was no way he could pursue the fugitives across the swamp with no light.

The chase was over.

Angela rushed to Woody. There was no pulse, no breathing at all.

"Let's go," Dag said quietly. "We have a long way before we are safe."

In the darkness they could hear the plaintive high-pitched cries coming from behind them. It was Farley's voice.

"Help me! Oh, God, help me! I think my back is broken. I can't move. Please come and help me!"

There was but one more ledge, then Angela and Dag would climb back down the other side of the ridge, and into the heart of Polecat Swamp.

Chapter 54

"What the hell were you guys doing out here?"

Vitilli's glare cut holes in Pauly, who was still feeling very ill.

"Where's Woody?"

"He ran off with the gal, I guess," Pauly moaned.

Vitilli paced around the campsite like an angry cat. Now he had a dead forest ranger on his hands. The pretenses were over. The lady cop now could bring charges, to top off all of the others that were pending out in the real world.

Deep in the woods, upstream from where he stood, a shot was heard, and some shouting.

Vitilli hoped that some witnesses would be shot, but by now he wasn't sure that even that would do any good. He had to think. Things seemed to be spiraling out of control.

"Who killed the ranger?" he asked.

"Abdul," Pauly answered with a groan. His stomach ached severely.

Vitilli shook his head in exasperation. The ranger's death meant nothing. It was in his plan anyway. But he hated the thought that things were so out of control.

"What were you doing out here?" he asked again.

Pauly seemed to be vomiting, and wouldn't answer.

"I hope the hell they don't kill that girl," Vitilli mumbled. "They can do what they want with Woody, but the girl might still be our ticket out of here."

Hostages! He looked at Mike, still doubled over with pain. Moving the injured man would only injure him more, but Vitilli didn't care about that. There would be no way he could be dragged out of the swamp.

Vitilli thought of shooting Mike, right then and there. But if he did that, Vitilli knew he would have to kill Doc too, and Doc was the only healthy hostage he had left.

Doc's demeanor created a serious dilemma. Forcing him to leave his patient and trek for miles away would pose a real problem. He'd seen men like Doc before. They were always stubborn, obstinate. They made poor hostages. They could not be bullied. They had no fear of what would happen to them.

Vitilli also worried about the weather. For now, they were still safe. It was hard to say for how much longer.

Another shot from the forest upstream! Vitilli wondered what was going on.

MacIlwaine and Abdul were returning to camp.

"Obviously," Mac said, "The fugitives are that way."

"Still," Vitilli advised his friend, "Keep an eye on the culvert."

Then he turned to Abdul. "Take another light, and go up the stream. The others may need some help, or you might catch somebody doubling back."

When Abdul began to do what he was told, Vitilli had one more thought, "Don't kill the girl if you can help it."

Screams began to emanate from the swamp: pleading, painful, desperate supplications.

"Oh God, help me, I can't move," was the pitiable cry, "My back is broken. Don't leave me here to die. Oh, please!"

It was Farley's voice. There was no doubt about it.

The cries continued, making for a disturbing background on a dark, cold rainy night.

MacIlwaine sat next to Doc, by the campfire and under the tarp, watching the culvert, with his pistol on his lap.

Doc was still tied, but he wanted to talk. He was incensed, and he had seen enough.

"Even in war there are rules about the way captives are to be treated," he fumed, "and these thugs you hang around with broke nearly every one!"

MacIlwaine sighed. "You might want to be quiet," he suggested quietly, "before we break another one."

A bloodied Martinson emerged from the mists, a dazed look on his face. He faced an anxious Vitilli.

The screams continued in the background.

"They're up there, somewhere," Martinson ranted angrily, as he gesticulated at the hill behind him. "I don't know where that girl got the strength, but she used a branch to knock us off the ledge. Woody's dead, we shot him. Farley's hurt real bad."

Then, as an afterthought, he added, "I was lucky to find my gun again."

"With more men, could we catch her?" Vitilli asked.

"I don't know, man. There are a lot of woods out there, and it's dark. I wouldn't know where to look."

"For chrissakes!" Vitilli fumed.

Farley's screams continued.

"I think she'll die like Boris did," Martinson predicted, all the while ignoring Farley's pleas. "She has no compass. She'll get lost and die."

"Or she'll come back toward here," Vitilli cried. "It's only logical. We'll fan out. We'll wait!"

To the others this was not good news. They did not look forward to spending the rest of the night in the dark cold wilderness.

More screams from Farley. Then a gun shot. And it was quiet.

In a little while, Abdul returned to camp, with the usual sullen look across his features.

"All that whining," he said perfunctorily. "The noise was getting to me."

253

Chapter 55

Waiting! Worrying! The feeling of absolute helplessness.

Police Officer Rose Fernandez sat in the darkness, listening to the ice pellets rattle off the leaky roof of Dag's crumbling little camp. She was damp and cold.

Things had gone so wrong.

She had watched as Mike Howell had been heartlessly kicked and stomped, and she had witnessed the way the thugs had humiliated Angela.

She had been horrified at Pete Randolph's impulsive move to rescue the girl, and his senseless death that followed.

She had stood helplessly in the wet forest, among the icy branches and stumps, without any means at her disposal to help.

What if she had still been a captive? Would they have treated her in the same way? Perhaps, in the light of her being a police officer, it might have been worse.

She shuddered at thoughts of what they might have done to her.

What had they intended to do with Angela had Pete not intervened? Would they actually have gone so far as to rape the governor's daughter? Certainly things had been heading that way.

She forced herself to think of something else.

She turned on the lantern, and carefully hung Dag's sleeping bag over the cabin's lone window. The window faced the road. Anyone walking past the cabin in the storm would be able to see the light.

Nervously she went outside to check. When she looked back at the cabin from the road, she could not see it. Thus satisfied, she returned inside.

She grabbed Woody's rifle, and removed it from its case. She wasn't all that familiar with ordinary hunting rifles, so she would examine it carefully, to see how it was loaded, and where the safety was, and so forth.

Six bullets! All that were in the case were six bullets! Woody had not left them any more ammunition than that. The weapon would certainly have limited value if they needed to use it. Perhaps Woody would have more shells when he showed up.

She sighed. Pete's pistol! The army of thugs had it again!

She imagined herself sneaking back down the road, and finding a sniper's perch above the Vitilli gang. She could pick them off, one by one, provided, of course, that Woody's sights were on. She had grown to dislike the thugs enough by now, performance of this act was almost tempting.

Of course, the idea was totally foolish. After one shot, they would fan out, and come after her in the darkness, with weapons superior to hers.

Six bullets for six enemies was pushing things pretty close anyway. Oh, how her mind did wander.

They'd shoot Mike or Doc if she didn't surrender anyway. This would probably be done in due course, but why rush it? Besides, they still had Dag's little revolver hidden somewhere, so hope lived on.

Again, every course of action she could possible think of had to be rejected, for one reason or another.

"Can't use you now," she whispered to Woody's rifle, and she put it away, being careful to store the six cartridges. Then she turned the light out again.

Somewhere out there, she thought, in the deep bowels of Polecat Swamp, Dag and Angela and Woody were probably wandering around, trying to negotiate a way to get across to where she was.

If they didn't make it, she would be alone. Alone to deal somehow with the Vitilli gang.

"Fate is funny," she thought aloud. She hadn't been out of the police academy for long, and actually had very little experience as a practicing law officer. "A few traffic tickets," she muttered.

Now, she was up against a vicious gang of fugitives. She did not know what they were running from, but it was very clear now that they all were deadly killers. She hoped and prayed that she would not have to deal with them alone.

The loss of Pete had been a great shock to her.

Unlike Dag, who seemed to be generally unable to share much common ground with the ranger, she had found Pete to be a very dedicated and energetic public servant. She could identify with his ardent passion for conservation, and he had clearly demonstrated his survival skills and his love for the wilderness.

Pete had been a private man, with a quiet, introspective personality. He had been hard to get to know on a personal level. But he had been a good and sincere person. That, Rose was sure of.

What if she had been the one that was armed? Would she have rushed into the camp site and tried to rescue Angela? Certainly sitting in the woods watching it all would have been quite cowardly. Pete could not be judged too harshly regarding his impulsiveness. He was doing what he had perceived to be necessary.

"I refuse to delve in hind sight," Rose lectured to herself.

She thought of Pete's family. Somewhere out there is a mom and dad who are presently comfortable and happy. They think their son is on duty now, but he will be home soon, safe and sound.

Tears fell from her eyes as she thought of the parents, and how they would receive the news. Again, she wanted to think of something or somebody else.

Dag! She wondered how the eccentric native of the north woods was doing. She could envision him, in the deep dark swamp, guiding his charges to safety.

She was shocked to realize that she missed him greatly, and she longed to see him soon. He was such a curmudgeon at times, she mused, especially when confronting those he considered to be insensitive to the needs and feelings of the Adirondack people.

"Just because we're outvoted," he had told her, "Doesn't mean we're not right." Then he had ranted about numerous wrongs that had been inflicted upon "his people" that he truly believed were "unconstitutional."

Anyway, Rose was a city girl. She had never given "upstate New York" much thought. In was just a colored portion of the map in her text book.

"Upstate New York" was another phrase Dag hated. "We're New York," he would say, "The rest is downstate New York!" It all amused Rose.

She felt strangely drawn to this gray-haired man whose background was so different than hers. When this was all over, would she see him again? Would they spend more time together? Would they try to understand each other's differences? Would they be friends? She certainly hoped so.

She tried to guess his age. Probably fifty, or close to it. He probably looked at her as a "young whippersnapper," as he would say, not to be taken seriously in a romantic way.

But she was older than she looked. There had been college, the service, working at a series of nowhere jobs around the city, and of course, along with all of that, the situations that had created her children and all of the trouble. Then came the opportunity to get her life in order: the police academy.

In spite of her seemingly desperate situation, thoughts of Dag and his contrary ways warmed her. Why was she so infatuated by this man?

She mustered an ironic chuckle. She had too much time on her hands at the moment. There were some serious things that had to be attended to, but she was forced to lay low in this little shack for many hours yet. She wanted to get on with things.

"I guess I've been in the swamp too long," she concluded, and she tried to brush her feelings aside.

She had to do something physical. All of the sitting and waiting was making her nervous.

"I wonder if I can get this stove to work," she said, stretching. Again the light came on and the sleeping bag went back over the window.

"Dag said to check the pipes, and look for blockage."

She also would check the pipes for holes. She didn't want to burn the little cabin down.

"A little heat would be nice," she sighed, "especially after they cross the swamp."

Chapter 56

The blackness of Polecat Swamp loomed threateningly ahead, and it seemed to be very lonely.

One couldn't see very far, with the rain coming down, but to Angela it seemed as if they were entering a dark abyss that stretched out there for infinity.

"Let's rest," the strange man who guided her said, and using the illumination of his flashlight, he waved toward a log that had been protected from above by a thick hemlock tree. It seemed to be fairly dry.

She was in shock. She knew she was. She had to be. In the course of three hours she had seen two men die, and had almost been killed by two more. Now she, a girl used to the finer things in life, was lost in a wet, horrible swamp, with a strange, hairy man she didn't know.

"My name's Joe Dagonneault," the man offered. "They call me Dag. I walked in here with the ranger, the police woman, and Doc."

A look of relief came over her face. She thought she had heard Woody refer to him. Still, she was wary. There had been too much violence, and too many strangers. Too many lies had been told.

"Angela Bartholemew," she answered, forcing a smile. She extended her hand, as a lady should.

"I'm pleased to meet you," he said.

She was surprised at the gentleness by which he took her hand. He held it carefully, and looked at her earnestly, and spoke with a soothing voice, as if he wanted to put her mind at ease.

"I'm familiar with this land. I spent a good deal of my life here. That's why they brought me, to be a guide," he assured her.

His tone seemed to be sincere. She desperately hoped that he was. She took a determined breath.

Matter-of-factly she said, "I have no other choice. I have to trust you. I can't get out of this swamp by myself. Without you I will die."

To him, she looked like a sturdy gal, a straight- shooter, one who would appreciate the truth. He thought it was best to level with her.

"I know the way out of here," he said flatly, "I know where to go. But it will be very, very difficult, and even with what I know, we may not make it at all."

"Let's get at it, Dag," she said bravely, as she stood up. "Is it okay to call you Dag?"

"That's my name," he smiled, "Can I call you Angela?"

She nodded.

261

"Then follow me," he said, jauntily, "We're old swamp crossing partners."

They had only gone a few hundred feet when she asked, "Do you think they are following us?"

"I hardly think so," he replied. "They wouldn't have the guts to come into this swamp, especially at night."

He tried to move ahead, and then shine the light behind him so she could see where to step. The ice storm continued to do its business, adding extra obstacles as it did, but Dag found moving about in Polecat Swamp to be easier than he had anticipated, at least for the time being.

"Of course, it's never easy to cross through here, even in the best of times," he reminded himself.

Her mind had been locked on the dead ranger and Woody. When they stopped to rest once more she wanted to talk about them.

"Were you friends with the ranger?" she asked.

"What do you mean, 'were'?" he asked. From his earlier post he had been unable to see what was going on at the crash site. He had no idea that Pete had been killed.

"The man they shot trying to help me."

"Woody?"

"No, the ranger, the one they called Pete, I think."

"Pete's dead?"

"It's a horrible story," she said.

"Save it!" Dag gasped. What a shock! "There is no time for long stories. Tell me later."

He stood to leave. The harsh news had given him a new batch of energy. Pete's dead? Unfathomable!

Several mixed emotions surged through him, as well as the recognition of the dangers they were facing. The young girl, Angela, seemed to be too young to be subjected to all of this.

"You saw two people killed tonight?" he asked, sympathetically.

"Yes," she answered. The shock was wearing down. She fought back the tears. She didn't even want to think of Mike, or Doc. There had been a lone shot back behind them a short while ago. That was more cause for her imagination to run wild.

Dag took several steps ahead, and when he looked back to light her way, he said, "The ranger was a fine man, strong and honest, and full of conviction. I admired him a great deal."

All of that was true. Dag had disliked some of Pete's beliefs, but he also had recognized that Pete was honest and hard working. "We were becoming friends," he told the girl.

After they had moved farther across the swamp, Dag had more to say.

"That boy Woody," he reflected. "I think he was a good lad, who fell in with the wrong crowd, and made some bad decisions. Every parent prays his kid won't do the same thing."

Angela was thankful for Dag's interludes. The environment was cold and damp and very uncomfortable. His conversation made it all seem to be less miserable.

Dag had reached an area that looked unfamiliar to him. He checked the compass and shook his head.

He could hear the gurgling of the brook, somewhere off to his right, but there were obstacles everywhere. The grasping spruces, hidden holes, and rocks to trip over were bad enough, but now they were blocked by a series of long dead coniferous logs, whose sharp broken branches crisscrossed to block the way, the sharp knife like projections pointed upward, forming a barrier similar to a chevaux-de-frise from an ancient war.

Finally they fought through until the black water was at their feet. The brook at last.

"This is our main obstacle," he told her. "We have to get across somewhere. To make matters worse, there is much more swamp to deal with on the other side, if we can get over there at all."

To Dag the water should have been moving faster. It all seemed to indicate a blockage somewhere. He would play a hunch and explore downstream.

"Stay here, I'll be back," he said. It was much more efficient traveling alone, especially if you have to retrace your steps.

Angela did not enjoy watching his light drift away, and he was nearly fifty yards from her when he shouted, "C'mon down here."

He had found a beaver dam, which could serve as a bridge to the other side.

It was the same deal. He would inch on out, then shine the light back so she could follow.

The footing was tricky, with sharp sticks to trip a person, and a slimy film of ice to slip on. With extremely cold water on both sides, they had to be careful.

"Damn!" she heard Dag say.

He had come to a gap, about five feet wide, where water rushed through.

"We'll have to jump," he said. "You go first."

He guided her past him. There was just barely enough room. Then he held the light so that she could see the rushing water and the sticks and branches on the far side.

"If you had to jump that far on a side walk in the city," he smiled, "you wouldn't think anything of it."

She was genuinely frightened. She was nearly frozen in place. She teetered back and forth, looking at the frigid water on both sides.

"It's okay," he said gently. "Commit yourself to it! We need to move on!"

His cheerleading helped.

"Hold the light on the other side," she said, and with a scream, she jumped. As she landed on the other side, a spray of water shot up, and sticks gave way under her feet. She fought for balance.

Success. She was safe. She felt a flush of relief.

It was Dag's turn. He tossed her the light. He had done this sort of thing a thousand times.

This time it was different. When he went to jump his bootlace, of all things, caught a long branch that projected from the dam.

He seemed to do a somersault. Then into the icy water he went.

He could feel the numbing cold run through his body as the icy water soaked completely through his clothes. He fought to grab the edge of the dam, and with a good deal of effort, was able to pull himself up among the icy muddy sticks.

He immediately knew what it all meant.

Hypothermia!

He fought the panic. He had to think clearly. He needed a plan of action, fast.

Finally he said, "Angela, come here."

She moved over to him.

"You'll have to go for help," he said. "I can't go far like this."

"We could build a fire," she suggested.

"In this weather, it will take too long. Anyway, I can try to do that after you leave."

"Oh Lord," she gasped. "What do I do?"

He handed her the compass, and pointed the light toward it.

"Go south. See the way the arrow points? Go exactly the opposite way," he said. "Now stick to that course. Don't be afraid if you think the compass is steering you wrong. It will be right. Go by what it says."

Chills ran rampant down his spine as the icy water ran down the back of his shirt.

"When you reach the edge, there will be a bank. The old railroad bed runs along the top. It is narrow, and winding, but turn right on it. Got that? Right! Okay, after a mile or so you will come to a ledge to the right. Go by it. Then you'll come to a fork in the road, bear left, or you'll go back down to the plane site."

He could tell that she didn't want that.

"A few yards more, on the left, you will see an old fire place and its chimney, next to a little pond."

"Yes," she replied, repeating his words, "a ledge on the right, bear left at the fork, watch for a chimney..."

"It's huge, made of big rocks, you shouldn't miss it," he said. "On the other side of the little pond is a big rock. Rose should be waiting in a little cabin behind it."

"And you?" Angela asked.

"I'll try and come along. I need to get warm, fast. You need to get help," he answered.

"But you'll need a light," she said.

"You can guide me to the railroad bed," he shivered, "I may last that long, but you can't let me hold you up. You have to go and find Rose."

Even Dag Dagonneault couldn't cross the upper reaches of Polecat Swamp in the pitch blackness. He had one slim hope to survive, and that was to get where Rose could find him before he had to quit.

The railroad bed! He had to reach the railroad bed.

Angela was a good guide, and she was patient. Crossing through the rest of the morass was a slow moving nightmare. As the time ebbed, Dag knew that the grim reaper was on his tail. He felt cold, lethargic, and indifference began to invade his mind.

Eventually, the bank of the railroad bed was ahead. The climb up on it was short, but steep. Dag was in bad shape now, almost played out. The desire to continue on had nearly completely waned away.

"Go on!" he said hoarsely. "Get Rose!"

Grimly, Angela nodded. She knew what her responsibility was.

As the beam from her flashlight got dimmer and dimmer, Dag struggled to reach into his waterlogged pocket to produce his cigarette lighter.

"My cigars are soaked," he mumbled irrationally.

He ignited the lighter, and the little flame flickered feebly, as he looked to the sky and watched the icy rainfall vigorously from above.

He heard a ridiculous voice from the back of his mind. "Maybe you can build a fire," it said.

He looked at the puny flame and the relentless storm, and laughed and laughed.

Chapter 57

The members of the Vitilli gang were played out.

Even Abdul seemed to be sleeping, although one could never say for sure. Pauly and Martinson made little mounds in their make-shift lean to.

Vitilli and MacIlwaine had sat up for awhile, trying to sort things out.

"Well, the girl is lost in the swamp," Bo said, "but I think that lady cop will be around looking for her. Maybe they have a place they intend to meet."

"The top of the hill," MacIlwaine suggested, nodding toward the culvert.

"Well, we'll check it out come daylight," Vitilli concluded. "We can't find anybody in the dark. At any rate, we're out of here bright and early, hostages or no hostages."

He took a hard look toward where Mike and Doc lay under the tarp, and he reached for his pistol. Then he shrugged.

"They'll keep until morning," he said, and he followed Mac into the tent. Pistol shots would only wake up the crew again.

As far as Mike and Doc were concerned, both were wide awake.

"Are you okay?" the worried medic asked from his cocoon-like sheath of sleeping bag and rope.

Mike, too, was tied to the neck. During the day he was normally free from the waist up, but at night the gangsters had concluded that he might pull himself around with his arms, and possibly set Doc free.

"Well, I'm not cured!" Mike joked sarcastically. "My legs wouldn't move before," he reported, "and a couple of hard kicks to the ribs didn't change things any."

"I just hope they didn't crack any ribs," Doc replied.

"I can breathe," Mike sighed, "that's good enough for me."

They laid quietly in the blackness. Nobody had added fuel to the fire for a long time, and the smoke increased as the misty rain fell into the dwindling coals.

"I guess the moment of truth is tomorrow," Mike stated, as if searching for something to kill the monotony.

"Yeah," Doc chuckled ironically. "Can you reach the gun?"

"I have it in my hand, which is across my chest. I'm damned glad they didn't kick it."

It was quiet for a while, each man in his own thoughts.

"What about Angela, Doc?" Mike worried. "Do you think she's okay?"

"I thought I heard Woody say that they had guides ready at all escape routes. We can only hope that somebody is with her now," Doc replied.

"This other guy," Mike queried, "the fellow who walked in with you. Do you suppose she's with him?

"If she is, you have nothing to worry about," There was an element of admiration in Doc's tone. "If anyone can lead her out of this swamp, it would be him."

Mike nodded as if Doc could see him.

"Get some sleep," Doc suggested.

"I don't know," Mike protested firmly. "If this is to be my last night on earth, I don't want to miss anything."

Chapter 58

It was completely dark on the railroad bed alongside of Polecat Swamp. Mists and curtains of icy needle like pellets continued to waft across everything.

Dag was alive!

He was sure of it. But in his semi-consciousness he was drifting about, almost aimlessly. He wasn't exactly in heaven, and he surely wasn't in hell. Even his concept of purgatory didn't work.

It was completely black, and he could hear the rains ruthlessly pelting something that covered his head. He seemed to be in a sleeping bag. But from where?

Gradually he was coming to. He was awakening from his nightmare. Had it all been a dream?

He recalled vividly his final moments: darkness, and uncontrollable trembling, then he had blanked out. He had heard that dying of hypothermia was like falling asleep, and that had happened to him.

He had left the world, but now he was back.

There was heat entering his body again, and the wrappings around him were dry. But there was a source of warmth, that touched his skin, and gradually the numbness that inhibited his tactile sensitivities receded. His awareness of the world around him began to revitalize.

Then it hit him.

He was in a sleeping bag with a naked woman!

In his mind he tried to paraphrase an entry in the first aid manual: "To save the life of a person who has lost considerable body heat may require, in some cases, skin to skin contact. Clothes would impede this process, and it would be highly recommended that they be removed."

Wasn't that what it said?

An old-fashioned sense of modesty began to creep in. Who was it? Angela or Rose? How long had they been here?

Suddenly he was aware of his hands. Certainly he was a gentleman, and there were plenty of places his hands should not be.

He tried to move.

"Dag!" It was Rose's voice. "Are you awake?"

"This is one great first date!" he cracked, covering his embarrassment.

"Can you walk?" she wanted to know, ignoring his levity. "We have to get out of here. Can you make it back to the cabin?"

"I think so," he replied, "if I had something dry to put on."

"Well your wish is my command. We found some dry clothes in your pack. I particularly like the boxer shorts with the little hearts," she teased.

"You and I may have clothes spread out all over the place in this sleeping bag, the better to keep them warm and dry," she went on, "I tried to tie each bundle, but who knows? Anyway, any time you think you're ready, we can get dressed."

"Our stuff is all mixed together?" he asked. "What if we end up wearing each other's clothing?"

Rose laughed. "Angela will get a kick out of it. She's back at the cabin, keeping a fire."

"Can I hold the light for you, while you put yourself back together?" he asked eagerly.

"I'm afraid it will be necessary," she answered, "but you'll have to keep your eyes closed."

"Fat chance!"

She quickly climbed out of the bag, and just as quickly had found her clothing and dressed herself. "I wouldn't mind standing nude in a nice warm summer rain," she informed him, "but this isn't it." She danced about and waved her arms, to ward off the chills she felt.

When she was once again snug under her poncho, she took the flash light from him. "My turn for a show," she said.

He was very lame. Moving, especially within the confines of the bag, was very difficult. In addition, he still felt very cold. He was anxious to get by a fire.

"Stay in there," she insisted. "Maybe when you get moving with dry clothes on, you can work up a sweat. We'll try a modified run. I don't want either of us to trip on anything."

"I've already tried that," he remarked. Thoughts of his bath in the beaver pond still made him shiver.

"I'm afraid you still have wet boots," Rose said. "When we get back to the cabin we can try and dry them by the stove." Then she added optimistically, "but you'll have dry socks to start with."

The sleeping bag moved about as he struggled within the confines to don his dry clothes. It was hard work, but the exertion warmed him.

"How did you get to be such a good camper?" he asked. "You can't learn all that you know in the Bronx."

She sighed impatiently. "I thought I'd told you about my combat training with the infantry!"

He was out of the bag now, sitting on a poncho while he struggled with his footwear, as Rose jammed their only sleeping bag into its stuff bag.

"Vitilli will be able to smell the fire!" The realization of the danger suddenly struck Dag.

"A chance we have to take," Rose said. "I've had plenty of sleep, and I'll be up early to stand guard. I know one thing, as soon as we're up, we're out of here. There is nobody we can help here anymore. I want to get to a phone before this gang of thugs get out of the swamp.

275

"You and Angela need a little rest, and to warm up, and then we're gone!"

She had brought two flashlights, making walking among the obstacles of the railroad bed easier. Even so, Dag felt that the walk was longer than he had remembered. Basically, he reasoned, it was because of his lameness and lack of sleep.

When they reached the cabin, Angela greeted them with a smile. The governor's daughter had dutifully kept a fire in the little stove. The three of them curled up on the floor together for warmth. All wet clothes were hung by the radiating stove to dry.

Dag kissed Rose on the cheek. "Thank you for rescuing me," he said softly.

When she returned his affection, she placed her lips softly against his. The act was spontaneous, and loving, and lasted for several seconds. It had been many years since Dag had felt the tenderness he felt right then.

"Get some sleep!" she ordered.

Tomorrow would bring a mad dash from the Couchsacrage.

Chapter 59

"BAM!"

The little cabin shuddered from the impact of the rifle report.

Rose stood in the open doorway, Woody's rifle in hand.

The startled Angela and Dag were suddenly on their feet, shocked into a sudden alertness. It was now dawn, and they could see a little bit.

"They're out there," Rose said with an agitated voice. "I just saw MacIlwaine in the road."

"I guess you weren't kidding about getting up early," Dag exclaimed, rubbing his eyes, "and a good thing too."

"Part of the job," was Rose's businesslike reply. Then, as if she needed to explain why she wasn't all that tired, she said, "I dozed quite a bit before Angela came to the cabin last night. She scared the hell out of me."

"Did you hit anybody?" Angela asked breathlessly, referring to the gunshot of a moment ago.

"I don't think so," Rose replied, "and now we only have five bullets."

This was a statistic that was very worrisome.

"How many men are we dealing with?" Dag wanted to know.

"There were seven at the plane site," Angela answered. "Woody's dead, and I don't think Farley is in the picture any more..."

"Five!" Rose said with conviction. "They killed Farley. I should say that the beast they call Abdul killed Farley. We're left with Vitilli, MacIlwaine, Martinson, Abdul..."

"And that little crud Pauly!" Angela exclaimed, anger from the previous night's ordeal resurfacing.

"Five thugs, five bullets," Dag observed, "and they have all kinds of weapons."

"All the more reason to make a run for it," Rose deduced.

"But Mike..." Angela began.

"We can't help him," Rose interrupted. "His only chance is if we can somehow get out of here to where we can call for help."

"He'll be dead before we can get help," Angela sobbed.

"We'll all be dead if we try to stay," Rose added, logically. "We won't need packs or emergency supplies. We only need the warm clothing we wear on our backs. We can be out of here in six or seven hours."

"I was thinking," Dag reflected. "Remember how Pete insisted that each break in the railroad bed be left with some safe way to get across? It's like he somehow knew we would be coming back through!"

Rose continued to stare out the window.

"There they are again!" she exclaimed suddenly.

"Grab your stuff," Dag said. "Let's get on our way."

"But they're blocking the road!" Now even Rose sounded like she was unraveling.

Dag sighed.

"Now what did you bring me for?" he asked whimsically. "Allow me to guide you to safety!"

The ladies could see that he was grinning.

Rose's worried countenance suddenly was crossed by a curious smile.

"Show us the way, cowboy!" she exclaimed.

Chapter 60

NEWS RELEASE (TV):

"Meteorologist June Barlow, with a WGHZ weather report.

"It looks like the storm that has inundated the Adirondack Park will move on soon. The high-pressure area over Quebec and New Brunswick, that blocked the air mass' exit to the east, has now deteriorated. The natural and normal sequence of events will be back in place.

"Sometime today, blue skies will again shine over The Couchsacrage.

"Get your rescue helicopter warmed up boys, soon you will be able to go and get the governor's daughter and her friends.

"Regarding a separate item from the news desk: No new information regarding the mysterious murder at a mom and pop store in Eagle's Aerie. A police spokesperson said, 'It seems as if all of the perpetrators have vanished into thin air.'

"It's comforting to know that Eagle's Aerie and the site of the crashed plane are miles apart.

"More later. Please stay tuned."

Chapter 61

"How stupid can she be?"

The smoke from the stovepipe had led them right to her.

Vitilli could hardly believe his luck.

Officer Rose Fernandez was trapped in the little shack ahead. She had to be alone.

Certainly the long lost governor's daughter couldn't have found this place. She had to be lost in the swamp somewhere. No doubt the brat was dead by now.

The only thing that bothered Bo was the rifle.

"We'll storm that goddammed shack, and take that gun away," he told MacIlwaine, "and we'll have that police lady for a hostage. What a break!"

Martinson was already back at the plane site, with orders from the boss.

"Pauly, grab the dead ranger's pistol. Bo wants us all fully armed. Take only the things you need. We're getting out of here and we're traveling light."

Pauly had been ready to go since daybreak.

"What was that shot?" he asked, curious about what he had heard about a half an hour ago.

"Goddam woman almost killed me," Martinson complained. "I've had nothing but close calls lately," he added, with thoughts of the night before.

"Bo wants us both back up there right away," he went on. "They've got the police woman trapped in a little shack. But she's got a rifle. Beats me where she got it. Bo wants to surround the shack and capture her."

"The hostage we need!" Pauly exclaimed.

Martinson nodded. He looked down at where Mike and Doc were tied. Both had ropes wrapped around them all the way to their neck. They were ready for slaughter.

Martinson then turned to Abdul. "We have no more need for these hostages. Vitilli wants you to dispose of them, any way that suits you. Then you can meet us at the top of the hill. If you are late we'll be heading past the rock ledge you'll see on the left of the fork. You can catch up."

Then he and Pauly headed up the hill, wasting no time at all. Neither one wanted to watch the sick Abdul do his gruesome work.

The evil assassin had already drawn his sharp filleting knife, and was working his way toward Mike and Doc.

Soon Martinson and Pauly had joined Vitilli and MacIlwaine. Martinson pulled the gun that once had belonged to Police Officer Jones, and Pauly now had Pete Randolph's pistol.

Bo and Mac carried the top of the line weaponry, automatic pistols with large magazines that could send many killing projectiles flying in rapid succession.

Mac crouched behind the large rock. When the firing began he would step out and pepper the doorway and window, preventing Rose from firing back.

To the right of the cabin, on the opposite side from the rock, was a knoll, high enough to afford a view of the roof of the dwelling. Vitilli and Pauly carefully ascended this small hill, to a position where they could shoot downward.

Martinson was to pussyfoot around the pond, until he had a position almost behind the little shack.

Slowly, like a constrictor closing its coils, they got closer and closer. There would be no escape route available for the policewoman inside.

When Vitilli opened fire, they all did. Splinters and tarpaper and glass flew about in all directions, as bullets permeated the tiny dwelling from all angles.

The plan was to shoot high, and cause Rose to duck. They didn't want to hurt her, but at the same time they wanted to make sure she couldn't shoot back.

"Stop!" Vitilli screamed, and the firing ceased.

MacIlwaine rapidly moved from the boulder to the cabin, and with a swift kick smashed open the door.

There was no response.

"Come out, godammit it!" ordered Vitilli.

Again, no response.

"Jeezus! You killed her," was Bo's conclusion, as if he hadn't had any part in it.

Suddenly MacIlwaine rushed inside, with a trigger itchy to turn bullets loose again if there was any sign of resistance.

In a moment, he was back outside.

"She's gone," he panted, "vanished."

A bewildered Vitilli descended from the knoll. The woman and the rifle were gone. But where?

"Another thing," MacIlwaine added.

"What!" the exasperated Vitilli shot back.

"I thought all the packs and supplies were down at the plane site."

"Yeah? What of it?"

"Well, there's a pack, spare clothes, and a sleeping bag in there."

"Let's go," Vitilli urged. It was all getting to be too confusing for him. He had no explanation for the extra gear. One thing he knew, "We gotta be out of here before any cop hits the main highway."

"And Abdul?" Martinson asked.

"He'll have to catch up. We gotta move!" the agititated Vitilli cried.

It was still completely overcast and the icy rain continued. The four thugs headed past Stanley's Peak, and down the road toward Bunchberry.

The cacophony of the morning's exercise had drowned out any other noises that may have emanated from the forest.

Chapter 62

NEWS RELEASE (TV):

"Bernard Gordon with a WGHZ report:

"There is growing concern at D.E.C. Ranger headquarters concerning lack of contact with the rescue party at the crashed plane site in the Adirondacks.

"A plane carrying the governor's daughter and two companions crashed two days ago, and at last report they, and four members of a rescue party, were all doing well.

"Last night's report, and this morning's report, have been unreceived, and attempts to make contact with this group have, so far, been unsuccessful.

"Spokesperson Bill Granger, representing Rescue Command, issued this statement: 'there is no need to be concerned. We have reason to believe that all people in question are fine. The geology of the area creates certain blank spots where radio and phone contact can be difficult. Our problem might even be caused by a meteorological aberration. We are confident that we will be making contact with the rescuers soon. We repeat, there is no reason to be concerned.'

"More later. Please stay tuned."

Chapter 63

Beechwhip Mountain.

It was not much of a mountain. It was less than two thousand feet above sea level, but it offered a stand of high ground that was surrounded by Couchsacrage swamplands.

Dag's little cabin just happened to be on its western slope, and attached to the rear of the shack was a crude woodshed, with a small door allowing access beside the old stove.

Dag had led Rose and Angela through here, and then he had pushed some rotten boards free from the fragile outside wall, making an opening through which they could escape.

He then led them up the hill, well before the thugs had surrounded the cabin.

The railroad bed had been laid around Beechwhip Mountain, following a course that pretty much stayed faithful to one contour line. Dag knew that a straight compass course across the top of the hill would bring them back down to the old road after awhile, and they would be headed out along the same route they came in on, and well free of the deadly killers who stalked them.

In the valley below they heard the thunderous gunfire as the Vitilli gang attacked the poor little shack.

No one spoke, but each thought of the rain of bullets that must have violated the shelter they had enjoyed just a few minutes ago. It was an incentive to move on rapidly.

After awhile Dag took a breath of the fresh, misty air.

"It's kind of neat to be alive!" he declared, "and the faster you move with dry clothes on, the warmer you get!"

"Well, I want you good and sweaty!" Rose remarked, as they hurried along.

"You say the nicest things!" he answered.

The beauty of walking on this high ground was a relief from the holes and roots, and the entangling limbs and blowdown of the deep swamp. To be sure, previous winds and the current ice storm had left a number of broken trees about, but it is far easier to step across a hardwood log than it is to deal with fallen evergreens and their numerous, sharp grasping branches.

The compass annoyed Dag. In clearer weather, he was sure he could have just walked right along in a straight line, but the visibility was still very poor. To go too far north of the omega turn would mean traveling parallel to the railroad bed instead of on it, and they certainly did not want to do that.

Angela's thoughts were on Mike. The act of leaving him behind, as she had been compelled to do, never would be resolved in her mind. She couldn't help but think that he was dead now, and to run from the man she loved when he was on the brink of execution just did not seem to be right.

The others had all assured her and reassured her, over and over, that her acts had been logical and practical. Staying at Mike's side to die with him, as the faithful Doc had done, would truly have been a futile act.

"But how can I live with this pain?" she asked herself, over and over.

It was certain that the day was going to be brighter than the day before. The rain even was letting up a little. Every now and then, another tree or branch would give in to the weight of accumulated ice, and crash to the ground, startling the travelers as they walked. Overall, though, all three sensed that the storm was coming to an end.

"If only this had happened a few days ago," Angela thought.

Then her mind was consumed by "what-ifs," but the conclusion of it presented to her imagination was a vision of a violent confrontation between armed policemen and the Vitilli gang, with she and Mike and Doc being held as hostages.

All of her thoughts were too grim, too sad. She doubted that she would ever recover from the feelings of remorse that she presently felt.

Just ahead, Rose was almost going too fast for Dag. He tried to engage her in a conversation that would take his mind off of his developing breathlessness.

"When we get to Bunchberry, what do we do?" he asked.

"You do nothing," she answered. "I'll call police headquarters as soon as I reach a phone."

"Newt Balanger's place," Dag suggested. "He'll be home."

"I doubt that anyone has any idea of what has been going on here," Rose continued. "The people of the world probably think this has all been pretty peachy."

"There are now a lot of dead people," Dag agreed, sadly. "Even the pilot's folks think he's alive and well."

"And Pete's folks," Rose sighed, "It will be a sad day when they all find out the truth."

"I feel sorry for Woody's folks too," Angela added, "I'll bet they are very good people."

Then Angela thought of Mike again, and the tears began to flow down her cheeks.

"C'mon gal," Dag urged her sympathetically, "We've got to move."

Rose changed the subject. "It hasn't rained for over an hour!" she declared. "Maybe we will see the sun!"

The thought cheered her.

"Look," Dag pointed. "Down below there. It's the railroad bed again."

Chapter 64

Clearing weather means increased visibility for all.

Had Rose known that the Vitilli gang was somewhere behind them, following the same exact route toward Bunchberry as her party was, she would have been very concerned.

But all three of them thought that the Vitilli gang was in their past, a horrible memory to be dealt with at a later time, hopefully in a court of law.

As far as Rose and Dag and Angela knew, the thugs were back in the swamp somewhere, fighting to get out in whatever direction they deemed best.

It was a new day, and as the sky gradually cleared, with patches of beautiful blue showing overhead, and the promise that the long lost sun would show itself soon. It almost seemed to be a beginning of a fresh start for everybody. No one expected that they would have to deal with armed thugs in the Couchsacrage ever again.

But they were not through with what remained of the Vitilli gang. Not at all.

Vitilli and his comrades were desperate characters. The mists had hidden their movements. Now it was getting brighter, and to Vitilli it meant police patrols along the highway, and it would be harder for them to hide.

To make matters worse, the cop, Rose, might get out first, and make calls for help. The highway might be teeming with authorities by the time Vitilli could find the road.

"Hurry," he screamed at the other three men. "We gotta move!"

Already he could see farther ahead. There were stands of spruces and alders and hemlocks along the way, and there were still plenty of ice-laden branches across the road. But what made Bo worry the most were long clear stretches where they could see an ever-increasing distance.

Up ahead, Rose and her friends had a different point of view. If you rush too fast, you risk injury. A slower, steadier pace was advised.

Rose marveled at how much easier the going was, now that all of the superfluous gear had been left behind. Then there was Pete's thoughtful contribution from the trip in: each time they came to a gap in the road, with deep running water beneath their feet, he had helped them build some kind of bridge across the opening.

They didn't know they were being pursued by ruthless running thugs who were capable of killing them in an instant.

During one brief rest stop, Dag looked quizzically at the policewoman.

"I've been thinking about last night," he began, "and I'd like to know when your next night off is."

She was curious about where he was going. "Wednesday," was her reply.

"Well, I would like to cook you dinner, at my place," Dag went on. "I think we should talk about us. Is there an 'us,' do you think?"

Her brown eyes stared at him, and he could see some moisture shining in the daylight.

For Angela's part, she felt uncomfortable. She stood up and moved far enough down the railroad bed to leave the other two with some privacy.

"I want to tell you something," Rose said softly. "When I was a senior in high school I got in trouble, I got pregnant. Not long after that my boy friend got killed on the streets in a gang war.

"Then, after I graduated, I was a single mom, and I fell in love with the most handsome and dashing guy. After about a year I realized that he was no good. He had fathered my second child, and then he disappeared from our life. He's doing time in Dannemora for armed robbery now.

"I made some bad mistakes when I was young."

She shrugged sadly and stood up. "I've stuck my mother with these kids through my attempts to get a decent job, through my military service, and this police business. My kids are reaching high school age, and I want to get settled and bring them to live with me.

"Maybe you don't want any part of all this. I owe it to you to tell you."

Dag sat thoughtfully for a while, and scratched his grubby chin.

Then he smiled, and in a hopeful, gentle voice said, "Well, is it a date on Wednesday, or what?"

Dag's shortcut across Beechwhip Mountain had bought some space, as did Vitilli's frivolous dalliance at the little shack, but the distance between them was getting smaller and smaller.

The only thing that slowed the Vitilli gang down was their lack of physical conditioning. Their method was to run at breakneck speed, then gasp for air and stop for a rest.

These rest stops, though, were brief. Vitilli's impatience would take over, and he would urge the panting men on, although, in truth, he was in worse shape than any of the others. That meant, that if he could will himself to hurry on, they certainly could keep up.

It was turning into a lovely day. Members of the advance group too, especially Dag, would get out of breath, and it was a matter of efficiency to take a little rest here and there.

"Taylor Camp straightaway!" Dag declared, pointing ahead. "You used to be able to see a long way here. The deer would yard up in that forest over there, hundreds of them. When we could come in here, years ago, we used to ride in on snowmobiles to look at them."

Dag no longer complained of how the use of this land had been snatched from him and his family and friends. He knew that Rose had heard enough of it, and that nothing could be done about it anyway.

"I hope the conservationists think they own enough land now," was all he said. "But I doubt it!"

Little did they know, that behind them, in that very same straightaway, the Vitilli crowd had emerged from the woods.

"Look ahead!" Pauly shouted excitedly.

MacIlwaine was carrying a fine pair of binoculars, which once had belonged to Ranger Pete Randolph. In a moment he was looking through them.

"Bo," he reported, "there's three of them. The lady cop, the governor's daughter, and some gray haired guy I've never seen before."

"Let me see!" Vitilli gasped, as he grabbed the instrument. This new stranger added to his vexation. Was he somebody they had contacted already? The paranoia had begun all over again.

"That's it," he declared, handing the glasses back to MacIlwaine. "We've got to catch them before they get out of here. They'll have cops swarming at every trail head."

"You think the main highways are still blocked?" Martinson asked.

"Road crews have been out there working their asses off since the beginning," Vitilli lectured. "And now, look, the sky is clearing."

It was his worst nightmare.

"I wish that goddammed Abdul would catch up," he complained. He already had the newer map stretched in front of him, and he nervously checked his wristwatch and his compass.

"Oh, hell," he angrily proclaimed, "There are only a few miles left. We've got to do something fast."

"Let's move on," MacIlwaine said grimly. He grabbed for another clip to snap into his weapon.

The thugs now began to move on the double quick. The need to survive was kicking in. Breathlessness could be overcome by a strong will. It was a marathon they had to win.

Unfortunately, Rose and Dag and Angela did not yet know about their pursuers. They continued to travel at their normal measured pace.

The stalkers behind them continued to close the gap rapidly.

Past Taylor Camp straightaway, the railroad bed wound around a series of small hills, creating a number of switchbacks. To walk these turns did not cover much distance as far as a straight line might be concerned. The path was sort of doubled against itself, and parties that might be apart on the road normally, were now linearly quite a bit closer to each other. To make matters worse, there were places where one part of the road was higher than the other, and a person could look down on the turn that was ahead of him.

The sky continued to show increasing patches of blue. It hadn't rained for many hours now, and the mists that had hidden the

Couchsacrage for days now lifted their veils to expose the rugged beauty of the primeval forest and swampland.

"You all be ready!" Vitilli warned his men. He could see the opportunity the switchbacks presented.

"Hostages?" MacIlwaine asked, as he wheezed along.

"If we get lucky, either of the women will do," Vitilli concluded, "but I don't see any need for that old guy, whoever he is." Then he added more, "Then again, I'd rather see those broads dead than see them testifying in court."

"That's for sure," Mac agreed. Then he turned to Pauly and Martinson. "You guys hear that?"

"Yeah," Pauly answered with a sneer, "Waste the old guy, stop the women. And if we kill them, we kill them!"

Chapter 65

Dag was thoroughly enjoying the walk.

It certainly was far more pleasurable than the trip in had been. It was a real treat to be able to see for a distance, and the brightness from the clearing sky added a beautiful glow to the spring vegetation. In addition, he could see landmarks that he had not laid eyes on in years.

Wonderful and loving memories passed through his mind.

As a boy, he had seen a mountain lion over there!

Joe killed a huge buck at that spot!

Sam's car broke down here, and got stuck in the swamp besides.

There used to be a very well formed twin spruces by this bend, and they were especially beautiful when covered with a powder of snow.

His mind wandered back in time as they strolled along.

They were almost to the big washed out culvert at Cobble Creek, where Pete had bravely swum across; to help set the spruce bridge in place. That had happened just the day before yesterday, but it seemed so long ago.

There still were obstacles in the road, to be sure, and they'd been negotiating around them for hours. Dag thought of how much easier this walk would have been years ago, before the road had been turned back to nature.

The tangled road took a series of wide turns, and then it dipped down into Neverending Swamp. Then there would be a long straight stretch, about a quarter of a mile, then Cobble Creek.

As Dag and Rose and Angela reached the bottom of the last wide turn, the Vitilli gang appeared at the top!

Right away, the thugs took out their firearms.

"Like fish in a barrel," Vitilli whispered.

Meanwhile, Dag was remembering an afternoon long ago, when his grandfather had shot a bear at the top of the knoll behind him. They had spotted the bear during a Friday trip to camp.

It was just by chance that Dag looked back that way, to relive the experience in his memory.

What he saw were ominous silhouettes, framed by the blue sky, their weapons gleaming in the sun.

"Duck!" he screamed, "Get cover!"

Angela was nearby. He grabbed her roughly and threw her on the ground behind a rock, and he fell down beside her.

They could hear the sound of the weapons as they opened up. The spray of bullets sent ice, gravel, water, and wood splinters flying all around them.

Rose had found shelter behind a log, on the opposite side of the road.

"We've got to move quickly," she cried.

"We've got to force them to chase us," Dag shouted. "When they come down off that hill, they will lose sight of us for a minute or so."

"We've got to get Angela out of here," Rose hollered back. "You guys go! I'll cover you!"

She already had Woody's hunting rifle in her hand, and she grabbed in her pocket for the five bullets that were left. The paucity of ammunition really frustrated her.

"Why don't you give me that gun?" Dag shouted back. "I know how to use it!"

"This is my job, not yours," Rose loudly replied, "and besides I outrank you here. Get a move on!"

Dag shrugged. There was no way to argue.

"Try to wind through the obstacles," Dag directed Angela, as if there was another way. "And stay below the bank of the railroad bed whenever you can. Give them as little to shoot at as possible. I'll be right behind you."

Angela was up to the task. Short bursts, from one cover to another, would present real problems for the shooters. She made a break for a stump, then a big rock, dove behind the bank, and then found a big hemlock tree.

The killers' pistols were for short range shooting. Already Vitilli realized that they had to move closer; bullets sent at Angela were falling short, and in spite of the steady spray he and MacIlwaine could provide, as the quarry moved farther away, the chances of success dwindled in proportion.

Pauly and Martinson began to sprint down the switch back. They had young legs, and hoped to pop out of the brush in time to do some damage.

Angela had already covered a considerable distance. Already she could see the Cobble Creek gap ahead of her.

Dag was quite a bit behind. Quarter mile dashes were a lot to ask of a man his age. He could run the short gaps to various natural barricades, but he had to rest often.

"Where the hell is all this fight or flight adrenalin?" he asked himself.

Rose had taken a more strategic route, stopping often to study where the thugs would have to appear. Her plan was to get across the spruce bridge, then she hoped that the three of them could pull it down into the raging water, creating a breach that the pursuers would find to be impassable.

She could see Pauly and Martinson now, about one hundred yards away. She hurried a shot, and the young thugs went diving for cover. She had missed.

"That will give them something to think about," she thought. She took advantage of their wariness and took off down the road.

She had four bullets left. A lot banked on if they could cross Cobble Creek and drop the spruce log into the stream.

Angela had reached the log by now. It was placed well below the level of the railroad bed, and anyone crossing it was temporarily out of the sights of the pursuers.

When she reached the other side, she needed to wait for Dag and Rose, for she was unfamiliar with the route ahead of her.

"This is too much running for an old man," Dag was telling himself, as he huffed along. He was nearing the spruce log crossing himself.

He was concentrating on Rose. "She should have let me have the rifle," he thought. "I'm familiar with it, and I know how to shoot it. Besides, I can't move very fast. She should be with Angela right now, taking her to Bunchberry."

He understood Rose's feeling of responsibility, but he was also upset that she hadn't settled for the best plan.

He conjured up another burst of energy, and bolted for the bridge.

His lungs were burning again when he dropped down to the log, but he was determined to join Angela on the other side before he rested again.

Then fate stepped in.

When Dag jumped off the log, one side of his left foot landed on a small rock, the other side hit the soft sand. The ankle rolled under him and he could hear a loud popping sound. He felt a raging pain where tendons and ligaments had torn apart.

He screamed in agony.

He hobbled to his feet, and in excruciating pain, lowered himself to the brook below, and placed his throbbing limb into the icy water. "At least I've got cold and pressure," he cried through gritted teeth, remembering first aid from his football days.

He also knew that his running was over for the day, and it dawned on him that it might be over forever.

Rose had no idea of Dag's injury. As far a she could see, her escape plan was going as well as could be expected.

She was now near the log as well. She sensed that Angela and Dag were safe. Now, if she could buy time enough to knock the log from its position, everything would be fine. She loaded the rifle one more time, shoving another precious bullet into the barrel.

She could see the bobbing heads of the thugs who were coming up behind her. She found Martinson in the cross hairs of the scope and fired. The bullet ricocheted off a rock near his head.

The attempt caused the gang members to duck down once more, slowing their progress, buying more time for Rose.

The straightaway was nearly flat, and Vitilli and MacIlwaine, being behind their comrades, had to hold their fire, lest they hit their own men.

When Rose dropped down to the log she could see Dag sitting by the brook.

Immediately he hobbled to his feet, and limped up the bank. The ankle hurt immensely, but as long as he could tolerate the pain, he could move short distances.

"I'm done," he declared. "I can't run any more. Give me the rifle and scoot."

"The log," she said. "We can drop the log."

"It's all iced in. We'd have to chop it free." he observed. "There is no time." He was not prone to panic, but his voice projected a lot of urgency.

"Oh God!" she cried. "There are only three bullets, and four of them!" She waved in the direction of the pursuers.

"I'll scare them away," Dag said. "They don't know how many bullets we have. And I can shoot that thing too."

"And I can't?" she asked curtly.

"Not from what I saw. You don't even know where the magazine is." Things were getting urgent, and he didn't want her hanging around anymore. "And you haven't hit a goddammed thing yet," he added tersely.

Her face was flushed with hurt and anger.

"Look," Dag said, more gently this time, "your job is to get Angela out of here. You can't let her die here, and I can't take her anywhere."

He noticed a tear beginning to run down her cheek.

"What's your job?" he asked sternly. His face was firm, and hard. "What's your job?" he asked again.

She sighed, and handed him the rifle. Then she handed him the three cartridges, all she had.

"Four outlaws, three cartridges," she sighed.

Then she looked up beyond the bank behind them. "That tree over there," she said, "will give you some cover."

"I will crawl over there," he declared. "You better get going. Vitilli's getting closer."

Impulsively she wrapped her arms around him, and gave him a hug.

"I love you," she said softly.

Then she scampered up the bank to Angela's side, and they were gone.

He didn't notice that she took one more look back. He was busily shoving the three bullets down through the chamber and into the magazine.

It was Rose's turn to leave behind one she deeply cared about, who now faced almost certain death. She looked at Angela, and they both began to cry, as they ran.

"That's the way he'll want to be remembered," Rose said evenly, "as one of the last of his kind. An Adirondacker."

Then they quickened their pace. There was only one small hope left: to get out of the swamp and get help.

It was a one in a million chance.

Chapter 66

"C'mon you sons-a-bitches!"

John Wayne had said that in a movie Dag had watched once, and it seemed to be the appropriate thing to say now.

Four killers, three bullets. But what if he knocked a few out, maybe the others would be afraid to cross, and he could hold out until help arrived?

He could see them approaching now. Slowly they inched toward the one-log crossing. He watched as they studied the situation.

"C'mon boys," he whispered. "Which will it be? Cross the log, out in the open, or swim the cold, swift, foaming water? Take your pick."

He worked the lever action, and the first of the final three cartridges slid into the chamber.

"I hope Woody had this baby sighted in," Dag said.

The rifle felt so good in his hands. It was exactly like his own baby, the one that his son owned now.

"Just like old times," he whispered. He cradled the weapon lovingly.

He didn't think that they noticed him, snuggled in behind the dark hemlock like he was. The tree had a large trunk, and he doubted that they could hit him with a frontal attack. His only problem was looking around it to see them.

He fought the urge to change the position of his throbbing ankle.

"It'll be swollen up like a cantaloupe," he complained. He wished for an ice bag and a place to elevate it.

Gradually the three thugs were lined up on the bank beyond. Sooner or later, one would be chosen to cross the log. Which poor sap would it be? Not Vitilli, that was for sure.

That gave Dag an idea. His prejudices against injustice took over. He had to try the weapon sooner or later, why not now? He had already picked the perfect target.

"If you want to kill a snake," he thought, "cut off the head."

Dag knew that a perfect shot required holding the crosshairs steady on the target, a gentle squeeze of the trigger, and a continuing view through the scope even after the gun went off.

"Blam!"

Blood immediately spurted from Vitilli's chest. The gangster fell to his knees, and he clutched at where the bullet had entered. There he stayed, gasping for his last breaths, as he died slowly.

The three others had dove into the swamp, out of Dag's view.

Dag was a little shaken. He had never killed a man before, and the experience had him a little unnerved.

"Give him no more sympathy than he gave his victims," Dag lectured to himself, "and that goes for the others."

He now knew that Woody had sighted in the rifle just right.

In the bushes beyond, MacIlwaine had taken command.

"I'll stay here," he said. "I'll return the fire, and try to keep whoever is there occupied. Pauly, you sneak through the swamp to the left there, downstream. And Hank, you go the other way. We need a killing shot at whoever it is."

The two punks slid down into the alders, and were instantly out of Mac's sight.

A barrage of bullets from MacIlwaine hit the bank on the far side, and some splintered the tree in front of Dag.

Dag held fast. He couldn't run, and he couldn't waste bullets. He searched for a target.

He fought to concentrate. He was constantly aware of the pain in his ankle, but he forced himself to look upstream and then down.

"They'll try to flank me somehow," he told himself.

He noticed some rocks in the gravel near his feet. "If I run out of bullets, I'll fight the Neanderthal way," he declared. "Anybody who tries to cross the log will get cleaned out with a rock."

He had always been blessed with above average peripheral vision, and to his right he noticed Pauly's red hat behind some spruces near a deep pool.

He thought of what Rose and Angela had said about Pauly. "He deserves what he's about to get," Dag thought.

Dag had to move slightly to get the rifle in place, and he hoped that he wouldn't be detected.

"I'll need a gun rest for this shot," he thought, and he laid the barrel of Woody's gun across a limb. "I wish I could see more of his body."

"Blam!"

Pauly screamed, and fell in the brook. He sank out of sight.

"Help me! Oh God help me!" the young punk screamed, as he surfaced, "I'm hit, and I can't swim!"

The current carried him around the bend, and out of sight, as Pauly bobbed up and down, alternating screams and gurgling sounds.

"Damn it!" Dag cursed. "I should have killed him on the spot."

He didn't see Martinson behind him. The youngster had been moving closer, using a number of broken trees as cover. Dag's change of position had left him exposed from the left. Martinson lifted up his pistol and fired.

Dag heard the shot, and felt a searing pain in his side.

Then the blackness overcame him, and he neither saw nor heard anything else.

Chapter 67

"Albany Medical Center. Fifth floor. Room 523. Easy enough to find."

Angela Bartholemew, the governor's daughter, was thankful to be free of the reporters who had met her in the lobby. It had taken two bodyguards to clear the way for her to get on the elevator.

She'd had enough of the receptions and the formalities. She was finally free to attend to some personal business and she hurried right along.

When she got to Room 523, she turned to her other two escorts and said, "I want to go in there alone!"

One of her men went inside the room briefly, and nosed around. When he came back, he nodded.

She pulled at the pretty blue dress that she was wearing to make sure she would look as presentable as possible. Then she walked inside.

The bed was empty.

Sitting beside it though was a man she had gone through hell with, Doc Ginsberg.

As he stood up to greet her, she rushed to his side, and hugged and kissed him affectionately. He made note of the scar on her forehead; the remnant of the wound from the plane crash. It had healed nicely, and somehow enhanced the beauty that was already apparent.

Then she stepped back as if to make sure it was really him. She shook her head happily, complete joy on her face.

"Oh Doc," she grinned, "I've been trying to get down here since I got home. It seems everybody wants to talk to me about what went on, and my dad's totally overprotective."

"Well," Doc said, "You didn't miss much. Mike's been sleeping a lot, and there have been lots of tests. You know, X-rays did not show a break, and there's a chance that he only suffered a bad bruise of the spinal cord. We may luck out."

"Oh, wow!" she exclaimed. There was reason to hope. Tears welled up in her eyes.

"Anyway," Doc went on, "you would have been extremely proud of him. I thought that Abdul was going to run us both through."

She sat down beside him. "I want the whole story," she said, "your version. I don't trust what I've read in the papers."

"Well, we were both tied clear up to our necks," Doc began, "and Abdul pulled out his knife and headed for me. For some reason he wanted to do me first."

The assassin had slithered to Doc's side, and had stood there for a moment, staring blankly, and rubbing his thumb against the blade, as if to check the sharpness.

"Did anybody tell you that you have the face of a camel?" Mike interrupted, breaking the killer's concentration.

"No, really. I heard that in your part of the world camel humping is a great sport," Mike had continued, "I'll bet your mother was a camel. I'll bet all you sickos who come over here looking for trouble are part camel, and part jackal. Yes! That's it! That's why guys like you sneak around and blow up planes and buildings and kill all kinds of innocent people. You're a goddammed cowardly jackal, that's half camel."

The whole presentation had an effect on Abdul. He moved away from Doc, and glided toward Mike instead.

"You shut up!" he spat.

"Look, Doc," Mike went on, "He's foaming at the mouth. He looks like a camel, and he can't talk without spitting all over the place."

Then Mike laughed efficaciously, as if mocking the man with the knife.

"Shut up," Abdul warned.

Mike's laugh was sarcastic now. "What are you going to do," he asked, "kill me?" Then he laughed again.

"It makes a difference how slow you die!" the enraged man ranted.

"C'mon you big hero," Mike taunted, "do it. I'm crippled, and I'm tied up. Looks like a fair fight for your kind. Do it, if you have the guts."

"It'll be your guts," Abdul warned, as he leaned over his intended victim. He reached for the ropes that bound Mike's chest. Whatever he had in mind, no one will ever know for sure.

In the sleeping bag, Mike held Dag's little pistol across his chest. He waited for Abdul to get just a little bit closer.

In the distance they could hear the rapid gunfire, as Vitilli's boys let loose on the little shack where they thought Rose was hiding.

At the same time, Mike was firing three bullets, into Abdul's chest and abdomen.

The ominous man shrieked in pain, and dropped his knife, and fell to the ground. He laid there and groaned for awhile, then he crawled toward the brook, and died while the water washed over him.

"And that's the story," Doc concluded, except for the part where I had to crawl through all the blood and gore to loosen up Mike's ropes with my teeth."

They were interrupted by orderlies, pushing a stretcher into the room.

"How is he?" the anxious Angela asked.

"Great news today!" one of the attendants announced. "They went after one of his toes with a probe. And he felt it! He's getting back some feeling!"

315

Angela fell to her knees beside the resting Mike, and began to hold his head and smother his face with kisses."

Chapter 68

Beep! Beep! Beep! There was some sort of buzzer going off.

Awareness! Sounds! Smells! He knew the smell. He was in a hospital.

He opened his eyes. It was sterile, and dark.

"Hey!" His voice sounded welcome, even to himself.

Yes, a buzzer! He could call for help. Where's that damned button?

He turned to look. His eyes were adjusting to the dim light now.

He focused on a button, taped to the frame of his bed.

Will my arm work? He gave it a try. Great pain!

"Well," he concluded, "not that arm!"

He tried the other. No problem, success at last.

The door opened. A fine looking woman in a neat, well-pressed white uniform appeared.

"Is this heaven or hell?" Dag asked her.

"It's about time you came to," the nurse replied, businesslike. "It's nice to see you too, Mr. Dagonneault."

She took the trouble to pull open the window blinds to let the bright sunshine in. Then she was gone again.

"Too bad she left," Dag thought, "I like her already!"

The long awaited awareness that Dag had suddenly demonstrated brought a flurry of activity into the hospital room. Suddenly the room was full of people. There were vitals to be checked, interviews conducted, tests to be run.

To Dag it seemed as though he had been semi-conscious before. It was all very vague. He couldn't remember much.

Now he was alert. They informed him of the extent of his bullet wound, including the gory details of his treatments. They even brought him up to date on his sprained ankle. It seemed at last that he would recover.

Finally all of the poking and probing came to a halt.

"You need rest," the chubby, bespectacled doctor said, and the entire entourage left the room.

The door opened again, and a man came through. It was his son!

"Dave!" Dag cried, "So good to see you. How did you get here? The roads are open?"

Dave laughed. "Dad, you've been out for several days! We almost lost you, you know."

The son moved over and gently took his father's hand. "Welcome back, Dad!" he exclaimed, his voice choking with emotion.

A certain elation came over the older man. "I should be dead," he said, "but I'm not complaining."

"You're a big hero," Dave laughed, "Wait until you read the newspapers! I've saved them all."

"The Bunchberry Weekly?"

Dave laughed some more. Dad was probably more concerned about what the hometown newspaper said than what was reported in *U.S.A. Today.*

"I saved them all," he repeated.

"How did I get here?" Dag asked, more seriously this time.

"Your friend, Doc Ginsberg," Dave answered. "There's no end to his talents. It seems one of his hobbies is radios. He retrieved two broken ones from the woods, and he found some tools in the plane. Somehow he put the two radios together until he had one that would work. Then he called for help."

Dave chuckled. "He had cops entering the Couchsacrage from every entry point."

It was all confusing to Dag. "I thought Doc was dead," he exclaimed.

"Not by a long shot," Dave answered. "He'll be here to see you. He'll tell you all about the adventures he and this fellow, Mike, had. He also wants to return an old family heirloom."

Immediately Dag thought of the pistol. "I hope he's got sense enough not to bring it to this hospital!" he declared.

Dag was euphoric about the news of his friend. He was especially curious about the radio business.

"What time was he sending radio messages?" he asked.

"By the time you got shot, there were already cops heading back in to rescue you," Dave reported. "They killed the MacIlwaine guy in a fire fight, Pauly Overton had drowned, and Martinson is in jail, facing capital charges."

"I can hardly wait to testify. Rose and Angela?"

"They are fine. Back to work, you might say."

"I've missed some funerals."

"Yes, you have. I hear the pilot's family grieved deeply. They thought their son was alive. And the Forest Ranger..."

"Pete!" Dag sighed. "He was a good man. We both loved the Couchsacrage. We didn't agree on how it should be preserved, and we were both passionately stubborn, but I want to meet his mom and dad and tell them what a fine boy they had there."

"A family named Woody want to talk to you. They said you were with their boy when he died."

"I would be honored to meet them. I'm sure they are very good people."

Dave held his father's hand a little more tightly. "I'm so damned proud of you, Dad!" he exclaimed.

Dag squeezed his son's hand tightly. He was choked with emotion, and words would not come to him.

"I hear that the governor will be coming up to see you," Dave was saying. "He wants to thank you in person for what you did to help his daughter."

Dag nodded, and then a wry smile crossed his face.

Right away Dave was taken by his father's devilish look. Something was going on there. He had seen that expression many times before.

"Now what?" he asked with a grin.

"Oh, I was just thinking about the state buying all that land," Dag smiled. "What's fair is fair."

Dave was lost in the reasoning. *Where is he going?*

His father continued: "I'm going to suggest to the governor that the state buy up parcels of land in New York City and Brooklyn, where Revolutionary War battles took place. This is sacred ground to us loyal Americans. Buildings should be torn down, and the land returned to its natural state, and given to the citizens as National Historic Parks..."

"You never give up do you?" It was a female voice, coming from the doorway.

"Can I come in?" she asked. "I hear that the most miserable, cantankerous old man in the history of the Adirondacks is here."

Dag and Dave turned to look.

An attractive woman was standing in the doorway. She was wearing a form fitting green dress that accentuated her lean and athletic figure, and the high heels she wore made her look taller, and even more striking.

Her dark hair fell to her shoulders, no longer pulled back as it had been when Dag had seen her last. She smiled warmly, and the sunlight from the window glistened from her moist dark eyes.

If it wasn't for her voice, Dag might not have recognized her. He remembered her in uniform, covered with a poncho, with moisture matting her hair and dripping down her face.

Now in the door way stood a strikingly beautiful woman, resembling a movie star, but with that same voice.

Dave was also mesmerized.

"Who is this person, Dad?" he asked. He had no idea about what adventure these two people had shared.

"I want you to meet a very special person," Dag was saying. "Very special, indeed!"

Then he turned to Rose and said hopefully, "I believe we have a date next Wednesday?"

THE END

About the Author

A fourth generation Adirondacker, Alden L. Dumas has enjoyed the outdoors most of his life, largely at a camp on leased property. A devotee of sound ecologic practices, he nevertheless sees no need for environmental groups to lobby for the purchase of "every square inch of Adirondack land."

A volunteer fireman, he was on duty during the great ice storm of 1998, giving a basis for this story.

He was born in Tupper Lake, N.Y. in 1940. He graduated from Tupper Lake High School in 1958.

After he graduated from SUNY Cortland in 1962, he taught for eight years in McGraw, N.Y., before he, his wife Pauline, and their three sons, Matthew, Jay, and Andrew, moved to Keene Valley, N.Y., where he retired in 1996.

Printed in the United States
1518600005B/46-168

9 781410 779663